FRIENDS OF THE
HILLCREST LIBRARY

©Maurice Sendak 1985

This book
has been donated
by

The ~~Sheey~~ Family

in honor of

~~Louise Tejeda~~

January, 1987

So long, Grandpa

BY ELFIE DONNELLY

Translated by Anthea Bell

✳ ✳ ✳

CROWN PUBLISHERS, INC.
NEW YORK

Originally published in German as *Servus Opa, sagte ich leise*
Copyright © by Cecilie Dressler Verlag, Hamburg, 1977
English translation copyright © 1980 by Andersen Press Limited

First American edition 1981 by Crown Publishers, Inc.

Originally published in the English language in 1980 by
Andersen Press Limited in association with Hutchinson Limited,
3 Fitzroy Square, London W1.

Manufactured in the United States of America
Published simultaneously in Canada by General Publishing
Company Limited

10   9   8   7   6   5   4   3

The text of this book is set in 12 pt. Baskerville.

Library of Congress Cataloging in Publication Data

Donnelly, Elfie.
    So long, Grandpa.

    Translation of: *Servus Opa, sagte ich leise*.
    Summary: A ten-year-old Viennese boy describes his close
relationship with his seventy-nine-year-old grandfather and how
he copes with the old man's illness and death.
    [1. Grandfathers — Fiction.   2. Death — Fiction.
3. Family life — Fiction]   I.Title
PZ7.D7193So   1981   [Fic]   81-3241
ISBN 0-517-54423-7   AACR2

For my son Stoffi

Michael Nidetzky.... Funny thing, if I write my own name out very slowly it looks strange. As if I had never seen or heard it before.

I know I'm wasting time daydreaming again, but no one's going to come creeping up on me while that vacuum cleaner's howling away.

Oh no! I feel a hand on my shoulder. I don't even need to look up; I know who it is. It's not fair. My mom just let the vacuum cleaner go on running, and here she is coming up on me from behind. And she didn't knock on the door. I've told her hundreds of times she ought to knock. I can't go bursting into *her* bedroom, can I?

"You're wasting your time daydreaming again...."

Well, I know I am, but this homework is boring. I don't want to do it. If I get to school early enough tomorrow I can copy it down from Lechenauer. He's fantastic at math.

Mom picks up my blotting paper.

"What on earth is the point of writing out your name on the blotting paper ten times in a row? You've smudged all the ink in your exercise book, too!"

How stupid—half my homework's all messed up. Covered with ink blots. Now I'll have to do it over again.

No need for Mom to say any more. I know I won't be allowed to watch television today. *Bonanza* is on, too.

And Mom doesn't say any more. She knows she doesn't have to. She just goes out again.

I wish she wouldn't look at me with that sad, disappointed expression on her face. I'd rather she shouted at me when she's angry, instead of looking sad. It's about the worst thing she could do, it drives me crazy.

No, I don't want to do my homework. Definitely not. I don't want to go out in the garden either. It's raining again.

I write my name several more times. Not on the blotting paper now. I'm practicing my signature.

It always comes out different. When Mom signs things, her signature looks the same on Monday as it does on Friday. But every time I do mine the letters are a different shape.

This time I give the *y* a big loop at the end of its tail. It looks almost grown-up.

Grandpa says you don't get your mature handwriting until you're at least sixteen. That gives me six more years to go. Six years, two months and three days. Quite a time.

Would it be a good idea to go see Grandpa? Maybe he'll tell me a story about the old days. Maybe I can see his collection of coins or look at his old books.

I tiptoe out of my room. Mom's in the kitchen. I can hear her talking to Frau Novotny.

Frau Novotny comes to our house every day to do the cleaning. I can't stand her. She has a high, shrill voice, like the whistle of a steam engine, and she treats me as if I were a little baby. "Micky! Micky, dear!" When I hear her screech for me like that, you can't see me for dust.

*   *   *

Grandpa has a little apartment in our house. Actually it's only a big room, but he always calls it "my apartment." He doesn't need more than one room, because he can use our bathroom and have his meals with us. Our house is quite old. It's exactly seventy-nine years old, the same age as Grandpa. He bought it when he was a young man, for his wife and his three children and himself. One of those children was my dad.

Our house isn't very big. There's just room for my parents and my sister and me. And Grandpa.

"People didn't need so much space in the old days," Grandpa says. He must be right, because his apartment used to be the nanny's room. That was when my dad was still at school, and the Nidetzky family could afford a nanny. Later on they couldn't.

Grandpa is sitting up in bed reading. I always wonder why he doesn't find the books too heavy. He has heaps of them lying about on the bedspread. My mom gets angry about that.

"Those books—they're so dusty! The sheets need changing every other day!"

I don't think Grandpa takes Mom seriously. Whenever she tells him off he grins at her, and sometimes he even puts his fingers in his ears. That makes Mom so furious she goes out and slams the door as hard as she can.

Grandpa is grinning now too, but this time it's at the sight of me.

"Not too keen to do your homework?" he asks, still smiling. One thing about my grandpa, he can read people's minds. He says he can tell what anyone is thinking from the look on that person's face.

I sit down on the bed beside him.

"Frau Novotny's here," I tell him. Grandpa mutters something and goes on reading.

Grandpa's room is the nicest room in the whole house. I think it's fantastic, even if Mom and Dad do say Grandpa's a bit crazy about his things. Grandpa is a collector. He has some of everything there is in the world in his room.

"It's like a junk shop," groans my mom. She can't throw anything away when she cleans the room, because if she did Grandpa would be furious. He's kept just about everything he ever got hold of in his life. Things he thinks are pretty, things with what he calls "sentimental value." He says every one of them tells a story.

A few years ago, when Grandpa was stronger, he used to take me to the Dorotheum. That's a very, very old and very, very famous pawnshop in Vienna. They have auction sales there too. Grandpa has a whole lot of stuff he bought at "Aunt Dorothee's"—that's what Viennese people call the Dorotheum.

"Worthless rubbish," says my dad, but he doesn't grudge Grandpa his pleasures.

I don't think it's rubbish. Grandpa has a big box with at least a hundred pairs of glasses in it. And old watches and so on—pocket watches and wristwatches and divers' watches, compasses and broken clock and watch hands, old voltmeters, binoculars. . . .

The writing desk starts in the middle of the room, where Grandpa's bed leaves off. It's a huge desk, almost six feet long and very wide, with lots of drawers on both sides. In the left-hand top drawer, Grandpa keeps a collection of old ballpoint pens and fountain pens and quills. And colored pencils and chalk too—everything you'd ever need for writing with. He's even picked up a pair of ancient old shirtcuff preservers, made of shiny black material. There are inkwells too, at least ten of them. One of them has red ink in it. I never saw red just that color anywhere else. It looks like blood, and it smells very peculiar.

Everything on the desk is all messed up. Grandpa brought his personal files home from the office when he retired. He used to be head bookkeeper with a firm called Reichert that makes binoculars and microscopes and camera lenses. Grandpa still has some microscopes. Sometimes he lets me look at things under them, but most of them are broken.

Grandpa has a brass bed. There's a potty under it, but Grandpa doesn't use it. And there's a big, dark brown earthenware dish with a lid. Grandpa keeps pickled eggs in the dish. If you hardboil them and put them in brine they keep a couple of months.

There are bookshelves along the walls, full of books right the way up to the ceiling. Grandpa has lots of books from Russia and Poland and Czechoslovakia. He was born in Budweis, which is in Czechoslovakia now, and it's called Budejovice instead. In the old days it used to be part of Austria.

Most of the books are quite interesting. I like looking at the old encyclopedias best. Grandpa has twenty volumes of Meyer's Universal Encyclopedia.

I like the old medical books too, but I can't help laughing when I get to those folded-up diagrams showing "The Human Body." The men in them don't have any willy. I mean, they don't have any penis. People used to be ashamed of it in those days. I don't know why. Grandpa says if God had wanted us never to show ourselves naked he'd have sent us into the world with trousers on.

I make Grandpa some coffee. It's caffeine-free, with lots of milk. Grandpa has a little electric ring near his desk, and a tap in his room, so if he wants coffee he doesn't have to go to the kitchen and listen to Frau Novotny. Grandpa can't stand Frau Novotny either.

He turns back the bedspread and pats the sheet. I quickly take off my shoes and crawl in under the covers beside Grandpa. It's warm, and I close my eyes.

Soon Grandpa will start telling a story. This is how we always start. First I have to get into bed, and when I'm all covered up he'll tell a story.

"Once upon a time, there was a boy called Michael Nidetzky," Grandpa begins. His stories always start this way. *"Hundreds of years ago he lived in Spain, where it is very hot, and he liked having adventures. . . ."*

I'm feeling very good. I snuggle up close to Grandpa. He tells wonderful stories. I'm always the hero, and today I'm Christopher Columbus discovering America. I set foot on American soil for the first time, believing I've reached India. . . .

I can see it all: me, and my men obeying my orders. . . .

Sometimes Grandpa's voice sounds very far away. It always goes quieter when I look at him for a long time.

I like watching him while he tells stories. He has such beautiful hair, all white and long. Grandpa doesn't like having his hair cut.

Grandpa used to have a beard, but Mom made him shave it off.

"When I put noodles in the soup you get them caught up in it. It doesn't look appetizing, and it's not hygienic."

I don't agree with her. It used to make me laugh when noodles got caught in Grandpa's beard.

The story's over. Grandpa was telling it more and more slowly as he got near the end. His glasses have slipped down on his nose. I carefully creep out of bed and cover Grandpa up.

He mutters something, and I take off his glasses and put them on his bedside table, so they won't fall off in the bed and he can't lie on them in his sleep. If he did that, he'd have to see everything through bits of broken glass.

I do that very quietly, so he won't wake up. Then I close the door and try to slip quietly back to my room.

"Have you been in with Grandpa again?" asks my sister. Goodness, she made me jump! Why do we have such thick carpets on the floor all over this house? It makes a person nervous.

"Yes," I say. I head for my room and my homework, which isn't going to get done.

"You're not supposed to go and see Grandpa before you've done your homework," says my sister. She says it so loud that Mom can't help hearing.

"Shouldn't tell tales," I hiss. Silly jerk! She says things out loud on purpose. Sometimes I wish Linda lived on the other side of the world, I really do.

Mom comes out of the kitchen with Frau Novotny.

"Michael's been in Grandpa's room," says my sister. She likes to act all grown-up, just because she's sixteen. As if being sixteen was anything special!

I couldn't care less. I go into my room and slam the door. Frau Novotny's voice follows me right through the thick walls. She's probably letting off steam about me again.

My mom is scared stiff Frau Novotny will tell the neighbors about the "awful things" I do. She'd have fired Frau Novotny by now—"But you don't find a cleaning woman as inexpensive as Frau Novotny in a hurry," she always says.

Well, let them talk about me! I wish I could live all alone with Grandpa. Maybe with Dad too. At least he isn't at home all day.

*   *   *

Dad tosses his briefcase into a corner.

"Hello there, Frau Novotny!" he says, smiling at her. Frau Novotny goes red all the way up to the roots of her hair. Grandpa says she's in love with Dad.

"She thinks no man can resist her, the old witch!" says Grandpa.

I'm glad Dad is in a good mood. That makes one

cheerful person in our family, anyway. As well as Grandpa, of course.

Dad sometimes spends half an hour or so with me in the evening. He calls it "confessional time." When it's confessional time I can tell Dad what happened during the day, the things that annoyed me, just about everything I can think of.

It's finally stopped raining, so Dad and I go out into the garden.

"Doesn't it smell wonderful?" Dad sniffs the air.

I say yes, I think it smells wonderful too. Though I can't really smell anything at all.

Grownups are peculiar about nature. We went on holiday to the mountains in the summer, and when the sun was setting Mom and Dad stared and stared at it, in such raptures they could hardly speak. The way they carried on, it was a wonder they didn't burst into tears. Though as far as I know, the sun sets every single day, right?

The garden doesn't smell nasty, but there's nothing special about the way it smells. . . .

Dad puts his arm round me. "Well, come on, then. What's the news?"

I can't think of any news. "You start!" I say, and Dad has to stop and think what to tell *me*. He tells me about someone at the office, and how annoying he was today. And about a new client who's really making life hell for Dad. And the way the cafeteria food is going from bad to worse.

Listening to Dad going on like this would stop anyone from wanting to grow up and go out to work. Grownups get mad about everything.

"Ah, well, that's why I'm so pleased to come home to all of you!" Dad says, beaming. Okay, but *I* don't think that's anything much to be pleased about. I tell Dad how I won't be able to watch television today, and how mean and horrible my sister was, and how Frau Novotny gets me down. And how I went into Grandpa's room before I did my homework.

"Grandpa is ill," says Dad. Suddenly he stops looking cheerful.

"What do you mean?" I ask. Then I feel silly. Ill means ill, that's all. "But no one would notice," I say.

"Not yet," says Dad. "Grandpa has cancer."

I know cancer is a bad illness. I've heard about it on television.

"Does it hurt?" I ask.

"Not yet," he says, still looking sad, and emphasizing the word *yet*.

* * *

This is one of those days I love the whole world. The sun is shining, there isn't a sound to be heard anywhere in the house yet. Except for Ignatius, who's my hamster. It's funny: every weekday morning I pull the covers up over my head at seven, because I still feel so tired, and the alarm is ringing and ringing as if it would get paid overtime. But on Sunday I wake up on my own—on the dot of seven, according to my red digital alarm clock. My stupid sister gave me that for Christmas. Sometimes her ideas aren't so bad.

For a moment I don't remember why I'm feeling so cheerful. Then I start to whistle—very quietly, so as not to wake anyone else up. I've arranged to meet Ferdi at eight-thirty. We're going to the soccer match. Purkersdorf is playing Hadersdorf at eleven. Of course we're backing the Purkersdorf team, they're our home side.

We planned to be at the clubhouse at nine to get our flags and streamers ready.

I put two heaping teaspoons of Ovaltine and two spoonfuls of sugar in my milk. Good thing Mom isn't watching. She's always going on about the price of sugar and the way I leave so much in the bottom of my mug.

Linda must have had the last roll, because the bread box is empty. Sometimes she gets up in the night and eats in secret. I get some cookies out of the box we had at Christmas, and read *Asterix and the Normans*. I know that book by heart, but I keep reading it over again, because I think Obelix is terrific.

My mom and dad are still asleep. They don't get up till nearly ten on a Sunday. I go quietly into the bedroom, without knocking. I'm allowed to do that on a Sunday morning.

Mom is lying snuggled up close to Dad in bed. I have a very beautiful mother. Especially when she's asleep.

I get on the bedspread and give her a kiss. She grunts a bit, and turns round.

"Mor'ing."

That's supposed to be "Good morning." She turns over on her other side. I can't help giggling. I put my hand in front of my mouth.

Linda is still asleep too—how that girl can sleep! Sometimes she stays in bed till lunchtime. Almost every

Sunday, that is; other days she can't, because she has to go to school, same as me.

My sister has taken to sleeping on the floor without a mattress. She says it's good for the spine and improves your posture. She read that in a magazine at the hairdresser's.

I listen at Grandpa's door. There's a rustling sound, so Grandpa must be awake.

"Come in!" he says. I was so quiet, too! I've no idea how he heard me. I burst into his room, give him a kiss on the nose, and then run out again.

Ferdi is standing by the garden gate, ringing his bicycle bell like mad. "Hi, pal!" he says. Ferdi's got a funny way of talking, like something out of an American comic. Sometimes he says he's got a speech-bubble over his head, but no one else can see it. Ferdi's a bit crazy, but he's my friend all the same.

I get on the back of his bike. I feel scared because he swerves a lot, especially when I'm on the back. I close my eyes, but I don't say anything. I don't want Ferdi thinking I'm a coward.

When we arrive the others are already there, except for fat Walter. He's gone to a Boy Scouts' treasure hunt. He thinks that's more important than the soccer match.

We go into our clubhouse, which is a hut we built ourselves in the playground near the soccer grounds. The mayor gave us permission. Our hut is a bit cockeyed. We didn't have any money for wood, but Herr Winter was having his old house torn down, and he let us have the planks.

By the time we've finished straightening things up

I'm feeling hungry. I've stitched two torn flags together again.

We go to the café near our hut and have some goulash. Except for Hansi, who sits behind me at school; he just has some sausage and fruit juice. He doesn't have enough money for goulash. It's only when we've finished eating that I think I could have lent him some money. I get a bigger allowance than he does. Or I could have bought him some goulash myself. Grandpa always says we should do as much good as we can in our lifetime, but it isn't that easy. Sometimes I simply forget.

* * *

Ferdi and I are feeling depressed as we cycle home.

The match was a disaster. Our team might have been asleep! We lost. We waved our flags and chanted in chorus for all we were worth, but it was no good—"Purkersdorf get / The ball in the net!" wasn't any use at all. Our side shot two goals, and the other side scored six.

"Soccer is silly," says Ferdi.

I look at him, surprised, because Ferdi is crazy about soccer. So far, just two things in life have really mattered to him: food and soccer.

"It wasn't worth it." Ferdi shakes his head. "I wasn't supposed to come today. I was supposed to go out with my parents and my Aunt Rosi. Aunt Rosi came from Graz specially, because it's my name day."

Poor Ferdi. I feel sorry for him. He gets hit when he

does something he's not supposed to. Grandpa says anyone who hits someone weaker than himself is a rat, so that makes Ferdi's dad a rat.

"Shall we go to the strawberry patch in the woods?"

"Okay, but only for a little while." I don't want to stay out too much longer.

We eat a lot of strawberries. The sun is low in the sky now, and I'm a bit cold. I feel as though I have to tell Ferdi something; I've had this feeling for two days.

"Grandpa has cancer."

"Whose grandpa? Yours?"

"Yes, mine."

"Bad luck." Ferdi spits out a moldy strawberry and grinds it into the ground.

"That's a bad illness, isn't it?"

"I think so."

"Cancer means crab, somebody told me. Wouldn't it be funny if you had a crab inside you?"

That makes me laugh. "Scuttling backward all the time?" I laugh even more when I try to imagine it. The crab would come scuttling up out of your tummy backward and come out through your teeth. It wouldn't know where it was.

"Scrabble, scrabble, scrabble," says Ferdi, starting to tickle me. "I'm Cancer the Crab. . . ."

He's pinching me now too. I can't stop laughing, I laugh till I cry.

"Stop it!" I shout. "Please, please, please!!!" I'm gasping for air.

We roll about on the ground in the wood, holding our tummies. They hurt, what with all that laughing, and the strawberries.

14

"Is your grandpa going to die?"

Suddenly there's something in my throat. Die? I never thought of that. . . .

Frau Novotny is always saying, "We all have to die some day." And, "Nothing comes for free except death."

I want to go home. We slither down the slope, and Ferdi gets on his bike.

"See you." And he's off.

I watch him go, feeling stunned. "See you."

My feet hurt, and what's more, there's a stone in my right shoe. I limp slowly home. It's nearly dark already.

Slowly, I push the garden gate open. I don't feel like going indoors now, but Mom has seen me. She calls me to come in.

"No, I'm staying out in the garden," I shout back. I head for my favorite place: the garden seat among the birch trees.

Oh, what's the matter with me? I don't like my own company. I stand up again and wander round the outside of the house. I stand on tiptoe and look into Grandpa's room. He's sitting at his desk, writing. At least, he *was* writing. His head is on one side, and I think he's dropped off to sleep sitting there.

I have to look away, fast. I've got a lump in my throat again. I wonder whether to cry or not. Better not.

* * *

Today it's sweetbreads and dumplings for dinner. I hate sweetbreads. Mom knows they make me feel sick, but she still cooks them, because Dad loves sweetbreads and dumplings. When I've eaten what's on my plate I get semolina pudding with cinnamon and sugar. It makes me feel like a baby. Not the semolina, I like semolina a lot, but all this silly business about eating up and then you get your reward. It makes me wild.

I push the bits of meat around in the horrible sauce. Grandpa nudges me and winks.

"Good gracious, look at that huge hole in the ceiling," he says in horror, and quick as a flash he picks up my plate and tips the sweetbreads back into the dish standing in the middle of the table.

I can hardly stop myself from laughing. I feel on top of the world now.

"Grandpa put Michael's sweetbreads back in the dish." Linda, of course. The silly jerk!

"Her mother to the bone!" says Grandpa bitterly.

"And what do you mean by *that?*" asks Mom sharply, though she knows just what Grandpa means.

I give Linda a kick on the shin.

"Idiot!" she whispers. Then she says out loud, "Do you think it's *terribly* funny to kick me, Michael dear?"

I see just how right Grandpa is. She does sound like Mom.

Dad taps his glass with a spoon. "Honored members of this family. . . ." He clears his throat. Everyone laughs, and Dad beams at us.

When Dad acts solemn like this, there's something up. I wonder what it is this time. Last time he made a solemn speech, it was about the new car he wanted to order, and we were to decide on it in a family council. Family council—I mean, how silly! I'm not supposed to know much about cars, Linda knows even less.

Grandpa is too old to have any say in the matter and Mom will have to get her driving licence before she can drive.

"Dear Erica, dear Linda, dear Grandpa, dear Michael. . . ."

Personally I think it's about time he stopped this joke. Grandpa taps his forehead.

"Oh, really, Father!" says Mom to Grandpa. But Dad sticks to his speech.

"From now on, the Nidetzky family are householders." Dad looks around, still beaming. Mom claps her hands, and Linda, Grandpa and I are puzzled. I mean, we already own this house, don't we?

"Yes, yes, I mean another one," says Dad impatiently. He takes Mom's hand and pulls her up from her chair. "We're going south—south —south!" he sings, acting just like a baby, prancing round the room with Mom like some sort of crazy kangaroo! I can't stand it when grownups fool around.

In the end we find out what Dad really meant. He's bought a holiday home on Gran Canaria, in the Canary Islands.

Everyone is very pleased except me, and I'm not so sure. I think of Karli Huber, in my class at school. The Hubers bought a country cottage. Before that, they used to go somewhere different for their vacation every year. Since they bought this cottage Karli has had to spend every Easter, Christmas and summer there.

So I'm not too thrilled, until Dad comes up with his second surprise: we're flying to the Canary Islands in a week's time to see our new house—right in the middle of the term!

"Grandpa will look after the house here for us," says Mom. "He and Frau Novotny will keep things straight."

"What do you mean?" I'm puzzled. "Doesn't Grandpa want to come too?"

"No one's asked me yet," says Grandpa, eating stewed apples rather noisily.

"Oh, but ..." says Mom, stammering a bit. "I thought—well, naturally you wouldn't...."

Dad comes to her aid. "The climate there isn't good for an elderly person—very humid."

"If Grandpa isn't coming I'm staying home too!"

The moment I've said this I could bite my tongue off. They won't really leave me at home, will they? Grandpa doesn't join in, he just looks at me.

"Silly boy," he says.

I'm sent to bed, the same as always when something has to be discussed and I'm not supposed to hear it. So I won't know what's been decided until tomorrow.

I think it's horrible of them to keep me in suspense like this. I want Grandpa to come too, I want him to, I want him to!

I wish a good fairy would come and grant me a wish, anything I wanted.

Should I try praying instead? Funny, I haven't thought of doing that for some time. I never pray in church on Sundays, nor does Ferdi. We just open and shut our mouths like fish in an aquarium.

I kneel down by my bed and fold my hands. I've forgotten how to say prayers. I try to remember, but nothing occurs to me except the Lord's Prayer, and "Gentle Jesus, meek and mild."

18

But that doesn't seem quite right to me.

"God, fix it for Grandpa to come with us, and get better," I say in a hurry, scrambling into bed. My heart is thumping, I don't know why.

*   *   *

Maybe the praying did some good, because Grandpa is coming too. It's a weight off my mind. If he weren't coming I'd only have Linda to talk to for a whole week.

I'm annoyed with Dad. He's too cowardly to tell Herr Mühlhuber—that's our teacher at school—that we're going to Gran Canaria. I'm just supposed to stay away. Dad is getting Frau Novotny to call the school the week we're away and say I'm sick, and Linda is in bed with a sore throat. When we come back Dad will write a note saying, "My son Michael has had flu and so could not attend."

That means I can't tell Ferdi anything about it: the new house, and flying there. The thing is, I've never flown in my life, and neither has Ferdi, and he's crazy about planes.

"Got out of bed the wrong side today?" asks Ferdi, grinning.

"Oh, shut your silly trap."

Ferdi doesn't say anything, but I know he's hurt.

"Look, I'm sorry. . . ."

I try explaining why I was so horrible. Because I was in a bad mood . . . but Ferdi doesn't want to know. I have to wait until the next break, and then I tell him all about it.

I mean, what's a best friend for? I can trust Ferdi

with a secret! At least, I hope I can.

Ferdi thinks it's fantastic. "What sort of plane?"

"No idea."

But I promise him a photo of it. And those little packets of salt you get on planes, and plastic knives and forks, and napkins and dried milk. Ferdi collects them. He's very proud of his collection. I'd like to collect something too, but I'd want to collect something unusual. I once heard of a rich person who collects islands, real islands in the sea. Fantastic!

* * *

Grandpa's excited. He thinks I don't notice, but he doesn't normally go scurrying around his room like a flustered hen.

"Look on the fourth shelf, Michael. That's it, up there on the right. The Spanish dictionary should be there somewhere."

He climbs on a chair and gets his old brown suitcase out of the wardrobe. The case is so dusty you hardly dare breathe anywhere near it, or all the dirt would go flying round the room. Grandpa hands it down to me—and of course I slip and fall! That's just the sort of thing that's always happening to me. Now the dust is flying through the air after all, making me cough.

"You'll have to let Mom clean this room up some time." I mean that seriously, it's not just because of the dusty suitcase. The picture of Schubert at the piano, over Grandpa's bed, is covered by a thick layer of dust too.

"Over my dead body," says Grandpa. "Well, she won't have to wait too long now."

I look at Grandpa, horrified. I don't think that's funny at all, but I don't say anything, because I can't think of anything to say.

Is Grandpa right? I don't think so. Mom isn't waiting for him to die! Even if Grandpa does get on her nerves sometimes . . . anyway, I'd rather not think about it.

Look at all those things Grandpa is putting in his case! "You won't need long underpants in the Canary Islands!"

"You never know. There may be a depression over the Atlantic," says Grandpa, wrinkling his forehead. I think he means it.

"Fancy me flying, in my old age!" Grandpa shakes his head in amazement, and chuckles to himself.

I like it when Grandpa laughs. He gets tiny little wrinkles around the eyes.

I kiss Grandpa on the end of his nose.

*   *   *

I enjoy going to the airport. I've been there three times before—each time it was when some aunt or other who lives in the country came to visit us. Dad likes showing the airport off to our relations. He's so proud of it you'd think he'd built it himself.

Our cases are weighed, and then they disappear on a conveyor belt. "That's the last we'll see of *them*," mutters my sister. She's flown once before, when she went to see a pen pal in England, and that time her luggage ended up in Rome.

We go into the restaurant, and I can order anything I like. It's funny, though, I don't feel hungry at all. Just the opposite: I feel a bit sick. Just a little bit. I almost think I'm scared.

And I'm even more scared of anybody noticing I'm scared. That makes things much worse.

Grandpa is holding my hand. As usual, he's the only one to notice anything is wrong. Grandpa has never flown before either, but he doesn't look nervous at all. He must have worked all his excitement off packing.

I'm sitting by the window with Grandpa beside me. He's still holding my hand. I wish he wouldn't, and I hope no one's looking at me. I don't want people thinking I'm a baby.

Mom and Dad are sitting in front of us, and Linda is in the same row as me and Grandpa. She puts on some bright red lipstick, looking in her pocket mirror, then she gets out a tissue and passes it back and forth between her lips. The red comes off on the tissue.

"Why do you put on lipstick and then wipe it all off again?"

"Idiot," says my sister. I really wanted to know! There must be *some* point in putting lipstick on and then taking it off again.

Dad orders sparkling wine, in five little separate bottles. After the first sip I feel warm all over, and I get a tickling feeling in my chest.

Grandpa says sparkling wine puts heart into you. He takes a big sip of his, and then another one.

* * *

I wake up, and at first I don't know where I am. I'm not wearing any pajamas, only my underpants, and I'm still dead tired. It's hot in this room. After a few minutes I remember everything.

I look round. This is the new house! Our holiday home in the south!

There isn't much to see. The room is low and white-washed, and it doesn't have any right angles, but I like it that way.

There's another bed beside mine, with Linda snoring in it. She reallly does snore, it's terrible.

Cautiously, I put a foot out of bed. The stone floor is cold.

"I sure did hit the bottle," I say, just to hear my own voice. I wish Ferdi had heard me—it sounded almost genuine. We practiced saying that a lot after we heard the way the gangster in the crime film on television did it. He had a stubby chin and striped pajamas and there were heaps of whisky bottles by his bed.

I don't know why we liked his saying that so much. I don't think being drunk is really very funny, and I don't like drunk people either.

Grandpa once said people like that are sick.

I must go and see him right away. I wonder if he's up yet?

"Don't make so much noise, you halfwit!" Linda sits bolt upright and glares at me.

"Silly cow!" I say, and I go right up to her and moo into her ear.

Luckily my sister is so tired first thing in the morning, she's hardly with us at all. She lies back on the pillows and goes to sleep again.

I pull back the curtain; the room doesn't have a door. This must be the kitchen. There's a huge round wooden table in the middle, and a stove, an old one, with propane gas containers in front of the window. Or rather, the other side of the window, because there's a ladder in front of the window, and Mom is up the ladder hanging red checked curtains.

"Morning, darling!" she says cheerfully. She climbs down the ladder and gives me a kiss.

Yes, I've slept well, and yes, I'm hungry. No, I'd rather have cocoa.

No milk? Oh well, tea then.

Dad staggers in past another curtain, dazed with sleep. Mom says he should put something on and not walk around naked, on account of Linda. Dad sighs, opens the case lying on the kitchen bench, and fishes out a pair of underpants.

"Where's Grandpa?" I ask.

"He's already up and sitting outside."

I look for the door of the house. Grandpa is sitting on a little seat in the shade.

"Whew!" I whistle through my teeth. This time, the view takes even my breath away! The sea is quite close, maybe a couple of hundred feet away, and it's shining—blue, bluer, bluest. Real sea blue. It smells funny, too. Well, it smells of the sea. Salty.

It's smooth as a mirror. If you threw a stone in the water now, I'm sure the sea would break into thousands of little pieces.

I sit down beside Grandpa, and I ask him isn't he pleased he came after all?

Grandpa hugs me tight. Yes, I think he is pleased, as pleased as I am. I run down to the water. I'm just about to dip my toes in when Mom calls to say breakfast's ready.

I go into the sea up to my knees anyway. It's not at all cold. When I run back to the house the sand sticks to my feet. Mom will be angry.

She is angry, too. She can't stand sand in the kitchen. And I'm angry too, because I think she might be less fussy here.

After breakfast I feel like exploring the village. Dad says I could get some beer at the same time. He wants to sunbathe.

I think I'm being exploited. Why doesn't he send Linda? Why does it always have to be me?

But Linda has been out on the beach for ages, lying there all shiny, frying herself to a crisp.

It's Sunday morning, there isn't anyone about in the village, and it's getting hotter and hotter. I wish Mom hadn't made me wear my red T-shirt. I take it off and tie it around my middle.

All these houses look the same. There aren't any streets, and the ground in between the white houses is sand and stones. I want to go barefoot, so I leave my sandals at the corner of a house.

At the far end of the village I finally find a place that looks as if it sells beer. There's a poster showing a huge lemonade bottle on the wall of the house.

I go in through a little door. If this is supposed to be a shop, it's a very peculiar one! There are two tables in the corner, with piles of food on them. All jumbled up together; flour, rice, eggs, olive oil, canned fish, lemonade bottles, wine, spices . . . but no beer. There are two shelves on the walls, holding packs of cigarettes and boxes of cigars, and there are tomatoes and green peppers lying on a huge sheet of newspaper under the table. And bananas in large clusters. When we buy bananas at home, we only get little bunches.

A fat woman in black comes through a wooden door. I realize I haven't the faintest idea what the Spanish word for beer is.

I stare at the woman, she stares at me. Then a little dumpling of a girl comes through the doorway. She is amazingly fat. She stares at me too. I stand there like a hypnotized rabbit. Finally, I pick up a bottle of lemonade from the table, and put it to my mouth. I pretend I want to drink it and say, "No, no," at the same time. I hope the fat woman will understand what I'm getting at.

It takes some time, but after she's shown me all sorts of bottles of red wine and white wine and brandy and mineral water, her face lights up and she pulls a crate of beer out of the corner.

I nod like mad, and put a note on the table. I hope she gives me the right change. I don't know how to cope with this foreign money called pesetas.

I'm glad to get out in the sun again. The fat woman said "Adios" and I said "Adios" too, and went out. Now I know one word of Spanish.

The fat little girl comes running after me and tugs at my trousers. She's staring at me again. I don't know what to say to her. I grin, feeling embarrassed.

"Christobalina," she says, pointing to her tummy.

Funny name.

I introduce myself too. "Michael." She claps her

hands above her dark head enthusiastically, and tags along beside me all the way to our house. That's just what I was afraid of. I'll never get rid of her now.

Dad summons up what little Spanish he knows and tries to start a conversation with her but he drowns in a flood of Spanish words, and shrugs his shoulders helplessly.

I slip away and go back to Grandpa, who is still sitting in the shade and dozing. Then I go down to the beach again. Dad is mad because the beer is too warm. He ties the bottles of beer to a piece of string, makes a big knot, and puts the other end around a rock, so the bottles can hang in the sea.

Christobalina has disappeared, and Grandpa is calling. I play a game of chess with him. Grandpa is teaching me to play; he says I show promise. Grandpa used to belong to a chess club, so he understands the game, and he can tell right away if someone has a gift for it or not.

*   *   *

It's afternoon. Linda is bright red already, and so is Mom. Dad is devouring Mickey Spillanes, one after another. I'd be bored stiff, reading nothing but thrillers the whole time.

Grandpa went to sleep while we were playing chess. He seems to be sleeping a lot these days. Mom says older people need plenty of sleep, but Dad says no, quite the opposite, old people need less sleep than young ones.

"Does Grandpa need all that sleep because of his cancer?"

27

Mom looks first at me, then at Dad, horrified.

"Yes, I told Michael." Dad shrugs his shoulders. "He'd have had to know sooner or later."

"But you can't just—a child—" Mom looks at Grandpa, worried in case he's woken up.

I feel hurt. What's Mom's idea? I'm not *that* young, not too young to be told things. And if my grandpa is ill, isn't that my business?

"Will Grandpa have to die?" I ask.

"Michael, people don't talk about that kind of thing!" Mom seems really angry now. I think the only reason she isn't shouting at me is because she's afraid it might wake Grandpa up.

"For God's sake, why shouldn't he ask?" There's a tone I know in Dad's voice. It bodes no good.

"Well, because—well, I ask you, Paul, is this any subject for a child to discuss?"

"Come off it! Who should Michael ask if not us?"

"And I don't see why you, of all people, wouldn't want to talk about dying, Mom. You just love it when the place is littered with corpses on TV."

That's Linda. Next minute, Mom will tell her not to be impertinent.

"Don't be impertinent!" says Mom. There—what did I say?

Linda is holding a lettuce leaf over her nose. She put it there so the sensitive little thing wouldn't get sunburned. She sticks her tongue out at me. Why me, for goodness sake? I haven't done a thing!

I don't understand it. Why don't people talk about dying? I decide to ask Grandpa. He always answers my questions.

"Ssh!" hisses Mom. "Isn't the sun wonderful today?"

I don't even have to look. I know Grandpa is awake now.

* * *

Later on Christobalina comes back, in bright red swimming trunks. I call her Dumpling, because it suits her. She's not so bad, really. If only she wasn't so fat. She has wonderful skin. Not as dark as a Negro's, but like someone who spends a lot of time in the sun. Mirko, who's in our class at school, looks like that too. He comes from Yugoslavia, somewhere near Dubrovnik.

Dumpling can swim very well. She shows me a place where there's an underwater cave, and the water is very clear. Dumpling dives for a big shell and gives it to my mother.

Mom is in raptures, because Dumpling is such a nice little girl, and she wishes I'd take after her. So polite and well-behaved. Except she could wash a bit more often, says Mom, glancing at her black fingernails, which aren't any cleaner now in spite of the diving.

Dumpling shows me a fisherman's hut that belongs to her father. He used to be a fisherman, but he isn't any more. There's only one fisherman left in the village now, and Dumpling's father works in a fish factory like most of the other men, putting fish in cans or something like that. I don't understand all of it, because there are some words I can't find in Grandpa's dictionary.

I walk some of the way with Dumpling when she has to go home. I shouldn't have done that, because halfway to her house her mother meets us, and drags me in there. She sits me down in front of a plate of something in red sauce and tells me to eat it up. The sauce is so hot and spicy it brings tears to my eyes. Dumpling gives me a sip of wine.

If only Mom could see me! I bet she doesn't know that even the children drink alcohol here. Though only at meals, diluted with water.

I go home before it's really dark. So far, Mom hasn't noticed that my sandals are missing. The fact is, I couldn't find the house where I left them. There are a lot of houses around this place. . . .

I'm worn out, and the soles of my feet hurt from the sharp stones. I limp, on purpose. I like limping. No idea why. Sometimes I just do it for fun. Silly.

Dad is in a bad mood because the tide swept his beer out to sea. Grandpa has already gone to bed.

I decide to take more notice of Grandpa tomorrow. He must be disappointed because I played with Dumpling instead of talking to him. Still, he was the one who went to sleep in the middle of the game of chess, not me.

It was fun diving with Dumpling. Sometimes you don't know whether to please yourself or other people.

Perhaps it's only because of me that Grandpa came to Gran Canaria at all. If I hadn't kicked up that fuss, I'm sure he'd have stayed at home, and then he'd have had to put up with Frau Novotny.

*   *   *

I'm lying beside Grandpa in the sun, with my eyes closed. I like it when the sun is so hot, I can feel my skin getting a bit red.

I've shown Grandpa the fisherman's hut. He thinks it's a good place, too. Right down by the water. I made Grandpa promise not to tell Dad or Mom or Linda about it; I want to keep it a secret.

I brought an old wooden chair out of the hut for Grandpa and put it in the shade, so he can be nice and comfortable.

He's drawing little men in the sand with his walking stick. Grandpa always carries his walking stick, even when he isn't leaning on it. It's wonderful: you can unscrew it, and there's an umbrella inside. If a lady comes toward Grandpa in the street he hides the stick behind his back. I think he doesn't want her to suspect his legs aren't as young as the rest of him these days.

"Take a look at those little lumps, Michael. There, among the stones, the little black things. Do you know what they are?"

"Tar?" I ask, sniffing. I crumble one of the little lumps between my thumb and forefinger. My fingers go blackish brown.

"It's oil from the ships," says Grandpa, nodding. "The big tankers."

I remember a TV film Grandpa and I watched together. It was called *The Plague of Oil.* There were hundreds of birds in it. Their feathers were stuck together so they couldn't fly any more, or look for food, so they'd have to die.

Grandpa says he was thinking of that film just now, too. And he sighs. "Strange animals, we humans are," he says. I think that's funny. It makes me laugh.

"No, really, I mean that seriously, Michael. We're mammals too. We may be the most highly developed

31

animals, but we're still animals."

I imagine myself sitting in a cage at the zoo, and monkeys and tigers going past outside holding food in their paws, saying, "This one is quite a young human, species Nidetzky, known as a Michael. . . ."

I laugh and laugh, I can't stop, I'm bent double. I try to tell Grandpa what I imagined, but I can't get it out properly, and I fall over my own words, getting more and more attacks of the giggles.

"Silly boy!" says Grandpa. When he says something like that it sounds nice. Frau Novotny sometimes calls me "silly boy," but she never makes it sound so friendly. When she says it, she really means I'm silly.

"I was only going to say we're the one species of animal that destroys its environment. And why? Sometimes I think mankind has lost its reason."

I sigh, softly. I hope Grandpa will soon stop, because sometimes he can go on talking about this kind of thing for hours.

Grandpa is sweating; he wipes the sweat off his forehead with his hand. "It's high time we started thinking harder, Michael. Not just for ourselves—for the people who come after us. For our grandchildren and great-grandchildren. I won't live to see mankind come to its senses, but one should never give up hope." Grandpa shakes his head. "It's your children and grandchildren who'll have to pay for the mistakes we make now, Michael. They have a right to live in a beautiful world, too. Don't you agree?"

"Yes," I say. Of course. Grandpa must be right. I wasn't really listening, but when he said "your children" that sort of stuck in my mind. My children. My grandchildren.

I can't imagine it. Me and some woman having a child, later on! No, I'd rather have two children. Me growing more and more, until I'm really big and all grown up.

And then I'll grow old. I'll get gray hair and pains in my legs, or rheumatism in my back. I won't be able to run as fast as I can now.

And some time or other I'll die.

I remember that I wanted to ask Grandpa something, about dying and so on, but it's odd, I suddenly don't want to any more.

"People don't talk about that kind of thing," Mom said. Maybe she's right. I don't know.

Grandpa sighs, and then he laughs. "Life should be a thousand times as long! Then one could do everything one ever thought of doing!"

He stares out to sea. So do I. The water's glittering. I'd like to be out there on the horizon right now, where there's a ship going by, a long way off. Sometimes I imagine I can see the curve of the earth. Can you really see it curving?

I listen to Grandpa, who's still talking. "Life isn't always good, Michael. In the war, for instance. . . ."

Oh, no, I think. If he starts going on about the war now, we could be here till evening. At least.

"That was a dreadful time, you young folks can't imagine what it was like. I lost one son, your uncle Karl—ah, well, you never knew him, he was killed right at the start. And my daughter Erna, she died too. . . ."

I know what Grandpa is saying now almost by heart. He's told me hundreds of times before, but he always forgets that.

"Paul, though, your father, he's done well. He's a good man. And you'll be another, I can see that already. I take a lot of pleasure in you!" Grandpa has such a loving expression in his eyes that I hardly know where to look. I always feel awkward when he says something nice about me. Perhaps that's because I don't think I'm as special as he thinks I am. And as I think he is.

He takes his shoes off. Grandpa always wears the same shoes. Black, and pointed, with long shoelaces. I look at Grandpa's feet. They're funny, different from mine. He has little white hairs on his toes, and his feet are pale, almost snow white, with brown spots on them like big freckles. His toes are crooked, like little claws, and there are thick blue veins showing through the skin above his ankles.

My feet are different. Brown and small—I take size 3—and not at all wrinkled.

Grandpa picks up my left foot. It tickles.

"They'll grow," he says. I put my foot beside his. They look funny together. A small brown foot and a big white one. A left foot and a right foot. I laugh at Grandpa and he laughs back.

"I'm old, Michael. Sometimes I'd like to be young again, but only sometimes. Old age has its good points too, it really does, you'll find out."

I help Grandpa, because he's trying to stand up. He puts his arm around me.

And it's different from usual. This time, I don't snuggle into the crook of his arm, this time I'm supporting him. Suddenly, that makes me feel very proud. I'm not sure why. Perhaps because I want Grandpa to know he can rely on me.

* * *

I'm dead tired when I get home. Dumpling and I have been out all day. We went up into the mountains, and she showed me a lake in the middle of the fir trees. It's really odd. There's the sand and the heat and the sea down below, and up in the mountains there are big forests of fir trees, and a fresh-water lake as cold as ice.

Mom doesn't mind that I'm so tired I could drop, she's annoyed because I'm late, and they waited supper for me.

"I didn't have a watch," I protest, but Mom is going on as if it were the end of the world. Don't ask me why. Sometimes she's very peculiar, but I love her all the same.

Grandpa is in the kitchen, reading a newspaper that is four days old. Dad bought it in Maspalomas yesterday. There are a lot of hotels and crowds of German tourists there. Dad told us.

I sit down beside Grandpa and read the paper too. He doesn't like that. He holds it so close to my eyes that the letters are all blurred.

"Anyway, there's nothing interesting in it," I say.

Mom dishes up supper. Stuffed peppers with tomato sauce. That's my second favorite food. Linda is writing a letter, and Mom asks why she has to do it on the kitchen table when supper is being served.

My sister raises her eyes to heaven and groans, "Oh, for goodness sake!"

"Say hello to your darling Gerd for me," I tell her. I can't stand Linda's boy friend Gerd. He's too silly for words. And his face is covered with millions of freckles, and he wears glasses. I know he can't help having to wear glasses, but I still don't like him, because he treats me like a baby.

"Idiot," says Linda. She can't seem to think of anything else to say. "Gerd isn't my darling!"

My sister turns red in the face when she's annoyed. She's red with sunburn already.

"He isn't?" says Grandpa, looking very surprised. "Then why do you practically lick his face off when he's saying good-by at the garden gate?"

"I don't!" My sister is the color of the red traffic lights now.

"Don't snap like that!" Dad is irritated. He was probably just getting on the murderer's trail. The thing is, Dad likes to read at meals and Mom won't let him. Not even on vacations. She just takes his book away from him.

We're in the middle of supper when Grandpa suddenly takes hold of my arm and squeezes it tight.

"Grandpa!" I think I shouted it quite loudly. I was scared, because Grandpa's face turned white as a sheet, and he was holding me so hard it hurt.

"What's the matter, Father?"

Dad hurries around the table to support Grandpa, who is almost slipping off his chair. He's holding his stomach with both hands now. Dad and Mom get him to his room and put him to bed.

"Did you forget to take your pills again?" Mom asks.

She calls to tell us to go on with our supper, but I can't eat another mouthful.

"What's wrong with Grandpa?" I ask Dad.

"I told you he's sick, Michael." Dad seems to be on edge. "He had one of his attacks. They'll be more frequent now."

"You would insist on bringing him along," says Mom, sitting down at the table again. "Dragging a sick old man on such a long journey! And to a climate like this! It's irresponsible, that's what it is." Mom's voice is getting louder and louder. "Suppose he dies out here? That'll make no end of trouble for us!"

Linda stares at her. "That's a horrible thing to say, Mom!" she says.

"Well, it's true...." Mom is clearing the table, making a lot of noise.

I can't say a word. I'm furious, more furious than I can say. Mostly I'm furious with Mom.

"It wouldn't suit you for me to die here, would it, Erica?" Suddenly we see Grandpa standing there in the middle of the room. Mom nearly drops the plates.

"I only meant the climate isn't good for you!"

"You think not? Well, never mind. I know I get on your nerves—you'd be glad to see me underground!"

I hardly recognize Grandpa. I've never seen him like this before. He looks angry—bitterly angry and unhappy both at once.

"An old person is just a burden to you, eh? Should I take myself off to an old folks' home? It would be more convenient for you younger ones! Thank God, there are still some people around who don't think like that. Look at your husband! And your children! They don't think I'm in the way—do you, Michael? Say something!"

"Oh, Grandpa!" The tears are running out of my eyes, streaming down, and I can't do anything about it. I just want him to stop being so upset.

Mom is white as a sheet. She's sitting down, and now she puts her head in her hands.

"Go to bed, both of you!" she says. Linda takes my hand, and we go into our bedroom. She sits on the edge of my bed and starts to cry. I can't bear to watch her, I've never seen Linda cry before. I mean, I have, but not this way.

I start crying again too.

I kneel down beside Linda and pat her arm. That makes her cry even more. It's a good thing there's no one to see us.

"Good night, Michael." My sister gives me a kiss and goes to bed.

Sometimes I'm glad to have her around.

* * *

I had nightmares. A pink elephant was dancing on my chest, and suddenly I couldn't breathe. I tried to reach a window. As I was doing that I fell out of bed.

It's about six in the morning, and I feel like a squeezed lemon.

I must go and see how Grandpa is. My sister's still asleep.

Grandpa isn't in bed. That's funny. He never gets up so early. His bed looks freshly made.

I go outside. Perhaps Grandpa has gone for a little

walk, or he may be sitting on the seat.

But he isn't there either. I whistle our special family whistle. No answer. I'm scared, very scared. I can see Grandpa's face in front of my eyes, the way he was looking yesterday when he was sad and angry.

My parents are still asleep too. I shake Dad.

"Grandpa's missing." I find I'm stammering.

"Nonsense," grunts Dad, not yet awake. "He's probably in the bathroom. Go and look."

But Grandpa isn't in the bathroom either.

Dad gets dressed very fast. He's scared now, too.

I wish I could get back into bed and pull the covers over my head. I wish I weren't here at all. I wish it weren't true about Grandpa disappearing.

We spent all morning searching. In the village, down by the harbor, along the road and in the next village. No one has seen Grandpa. Mom is crying her eyes out, using tissue after tissue to blow her nose. She says she's afraid Grandpa may do himself some harm. He might walk into the sea until he's out of his depth.

Grandpa can't swim.

"It's all my fault," sobs Mom. Dad wants to drive to the police station. It's two o'clock by now, and I'm hungry. We haven't had anything to eat yet today. No breakfast or lunch.

Linda is sitting indoors reading. She says if she comes to help look for Grandpa she'll get hysterical.

Dumpling's mother has started praying. My heart is beating louder than usual, and much faster. Suppose we don't find him? Crazy ideas come into my head. Perhaps someone has kidnapped Grandpa.

I plod through the sand. Why does Mom think

Grandpa would want to do himself harm? I can't imagine anyone killing himself. Why would you want to do that? And how would you do it? It must hurt. I read in the paper about someone who cut his wrists.

I can't stand pain. I even start yelling when Mom takes a Band-Aid off me.

I think you'd have to be very sad not to want to live any more. I couldn't ever be that sad. But could Grandpa?

I shake my head.

"No," I tell myself, out loud. No, Grandpa couldn't ever be that sad, either. Grandpa is always cheerful, even when he's a little sad.

I start running. I feel I must run, race, go faster and faster, fast as an arrow. I feel the air dividing as I run; the wind whistles round my ears.

Gasping for breath, I come to a halt outside the fisherman's hut and throw myself on the sand. Then I spit. I forgot to close my mouth, and now it's full of sand.

"Come in, Michael."

It's Grandpa. In the hut. I'm laughing and crying both at once.

What an idiot I am! Imagine not thinking of that! We looked everywhere except in the hut.

Grandpa is doing crossword puzzles. I hug him, practically squashing him. Still breathless, I tell him how Mom and Dad are looking for him, and Dad wants to go to the police, and Linda's so upset she can't do anything but read, and Mom is in hysterics because she thinks Grandpa's killed himself and it's her fault.

"I only wanted a bit of peace," says Grandpa. "That's all." They can go on worrying about him a bit longer, he adds. That makes me angry, because I don't think it's fair. After all, Mom and Dad are scared and worried.

But he doesn't want to go home.

"You can go and tell them, but I'm staying here. I'll be staying here in any event."

He bends over his crossword puzzle again and writes in several letters, very neatly.

"What do you mean?"

"Staying for good," he says.

I'm baffled. I don't know what to say.

"Look, I'll tell Dad it's all right." I run back to the house.

Linda is red-eyed from crying, and we go to find Mom and Dad together.

Mom is furious. She says it was "disgraceful" of Grandpa to go off like that. "Shocking lack of consideration! After all I've done for him."

I have to take my parents and show them where Grandpa is. Our hut isn't a secret any more. Not that it matters; we're going home anyway the day after tomorrow.

"Father, dear!" Mom flings herself on Grandpa and says he shouldn't have done such a thing to her. Grandpa has folded his arms; he's keeping quiet.

"Well, you certainly scared us!" says Dad, laughing. Grandpa still keeps quiet.

"Say something, please!" Mom begs.

"I want to be left in peace." Grandpa goes on with his crossword puzzle.

"I'll cook you something really nice for supper today—anything you like," Mom tempts him.

"I'm going to move in here."

Then Mom tells Grandpa he's crazy.

"Very well, I'm crazy. At least I won't be making any more work for you," he says. "You ought to be glad of that."

But Mom doesn't seem at all glad. She starts telling him off.

"I'm staying here," he says. "I don't want to go home with you. I'll have my pension sent out to me—an old man like me, what more could I wish for? Sunshine, a little hut to live in, and I'm sure Christobalina's mother will look after me very nicely for a few pesetas a day."

Mom clasps her hands above her head and says that Grandpa has gone completely out of his mind.

"You think so? I don't," says Grandpa. "And now I really would like to be left in peace to do my crossword. Name of Beethoven's Third Symphony in E-flat major?"

"Eroica," says Dad. "Look, Father, be reasonable. Please!"

"No." Grandpa doesn't even look up. "I'd like Michael to bring me my case."

"Yes, Grandpa."

"Certainly not. I'm not having my son run about after such an obstinate old fool," says Mom, crossly. "Come along, Michael, we're going now." And she drags me out of the hut and slams its door, making the walls shake.

*   *   *

I don't know what to do. Mom said I wasn't to take Grandpa his case, but I'd promised him I would.

In a way I think all this is exciting. Grandpa is a real adventurer now. It's very brave of him, planning to stay here.

But I know he'll come home with us in the end. Because I want him to, and Grandpa won't let me down.

He's gone on to the next puzzle now. I put the case down. It was heavy, and I'm out of breath.

"You're not really going to stay here, are you?" I ask, kneeling on the seat beside Grandpa.

"Why not? It's delightful here. Paradise. And I only have a few months left to me. I'd like to spend them in peace, that's all I ask for."

"What do you mean, a few months left? What happens after that?"

"Then I grow a pair of wings and turn into an angel!" Grandpa laughs. "Well, no, Michael—but I certainly won't live longer than a few months."

"How do you know?" I ask. "I mean, no one can know that, can they?"

Grandpa says he can feel it. "Your grandma felt it too. She knew very well when she only had a few weeks to live—back in '59, that was."

I don't believe it. How can you feel sure you're going to die?

"Ah, there are a lot of things one can't imagine," says Grandpa. "Especially when one's as young as you are."

Suddenly I remember something I once read. In the *Jungle Book,* I think. About elephants knowing they're about to die, and then they leave their herd and go to a place with a lot of elephant skeletons lying around. An elephants' graveyard. And they die there.

Does Grandpa want to go away from us, like that, so as to die in peace?

"It's a funny thing"—Grandpa is cleaning his glasses on his shirt tail—"me getting this in my liver. They say that only happens to someone who's been a heavy drinker all his life. And all I've ever drunk is the odd glass of wine."

I'm tired.

"Grandpa, please come home with me."

I beg Grandpa to come; I look at him as winningly as I can. At least, I try to. Do I really look winning when I think I'm looking winning? I've never tried it out in front of a mirror. Still, I hope Grandpa is impressed.

"Don't squint, Michael!" he says. "It's bad for the eyes."

*   *   *

Don't ask me why I'm always late for school. I don't know either. The bell is ringing as I run up the stairs like a scalded cat.

"Hi," whispers Ferdi. He has to whisper because Herr Mühlhuber is coming into the classroom right behind me.

"Flu, eh?" asks Herr Mühlhuber, when I put my absence note on his desk.

"Yes." I can feel the way he's looking at me. I know how tanned I got last week.

A week. Time's a funny thing. It isn't always the same length—at least, that's how it strikes me. For instance, a week on vacation is much shorter than a week

44

of school with two dictations and one test on describing a picture in your own words.

On the other hand, that week on vacation is incredibly long when you're in the middle of it. It doesn't start shrinking until you're going home again. Crazy, really.

At recess, I tell Ferdi all about Gran Canaria. "And your grandpa ran away," he says.

I'm staggered. How does he know that?

"Erwin told me. Gerd's brother—you know Gerd: your sister's boy friend. He lives near us."

Linda can't keep her mouth shut even for ten minutes. We didn't get home till yesterday evening, and she disappeared while we were still unpacking our cases. Right off to see her darling Gerd.

I tell Ferdi exactly what happened.

"I feel sorry for your grandpa," he says thoughtfully.

Ferdi gives me his chewing gum in return for the little packet of salt and plastic cutlery from the plane. It isn't new, and he's already chewed all the flavor out, but I take it all the same.

"Good thing your grandpa came home with you."

Yes. I think so too.

After school Ferdi walks home with me. I'm just opening the garden gate when a car comes round the corner. It's a dark blue Peugeot, with a red and white sticker saying "Doctor on Call" in the window.

Dr. Gnad gets out. "Well, how's life, Michael?"

I like Dr. Gnad. He's known me ever since I was born. Grandpa says he's the best doctor for miles around, because he always takes his time with his patients. And Mom says there isn't another doctor to compare with

Dr. Gnad in all Austria. "One of the old kind, a real family doctor."

Once, Mom had something the matter with her circulation, and the doctor came in the middle of the night and stayed beside her bed after he gave her an injection. He held her hand till she went to sleep. He can tell a whole lot of stories about his travels, too. He's been almost all over the world.

"Fine, thanks," I say.

I'm always polite to him. Frau Novotny once told me you must always be polite to a doctor and respect him, because he's spent so long studying, and that makes him very smart.

"Rubbish," said Dr. Gnad, who happened to hear her say this at the time. "You must trust me, that's all you have to do."

"And have a health insurance card," whispered Frau Novotny, who can't let well enough alone.

"How's your grandpa?" Dr. Gnad is asking me now. "Did he stick to his diet on vacation?"

Diet? I didn't notice any diet. Grandpa always ate whatever the rest of us were having.

"He had one of his attacks once, when it was stuffed peppers for supper."

"Hm . . . well, we'll have to see about that," says Dr. Gnad, looking fierce. I wouldn't like to be in Grandpa's shoes.

I go to see Mom in the kitchen and ask if she knew anything about a diet. She didn't.

Frau Novotny pricks up her ears. Dear me, has Grandpa been keeping something secret from us?

Goodness, no, says Mom on the defensive. She doesn't

want Frau Novotny gossiping. Mom really hates to think of people talking about us.

* * *

"I'm going to have to steal your grandpa for a few days." Dr. Gnad puts his hand on my shoulder. "I must send him to hospital for an examination."

"What's the matter with Herr Nidetzky, doctor?" Frau Novotny comes through the kitchen door, wiping her hands on a dishtowel, full of curiosity and staring at the doctor.

"Nothing to speak of, Frau Novotny."

She goes to clean the doctor's house twice a week, too, that's how he knows her.

"It's a medical secret," I say, grinning. Frau Novotny tells me not to be sassy.

Dr. Gnad goes into the kitchen to see Mom, and closes the door firmly behind him. Frau Novotny is left outside, with me.

"Well, fancy that!" Frau Novotny takes a deep breath. She is not pleased.

The door opens again, and the doctor says he wants a word with me. We go into the garden. "Your mother tells me you know what the trouble is?"

I nod.

"Yes, well; your grandpa isn't very well. He must go into hospital for another thorough examination— would you like to help me, Michael?"

"Oh, yes," I say at once.

"Then remind your grandpa to take his pills—regularly! And not to eat anything he shouldn't. I've given your mother his diet sheet."

"I'll remember." I'm longing to know more, I'd like to know how much longer Grandpa will live, but suddenly I can't get another word out.

"Then—"

I'm trying to keep the tears back, but Dr. Gnad has sharp eyes.

"Don't cry, Michael. Come on, you're a big boy now!"

"It's all right." I swallow once or twice—and then that stupid lump in my throat really does go away.

*   *   *

I stop in the doorway, and I can't help laughing. Because outside the door I was thinking Grandpa would be sitting up in bed *just* like that, with his glasses *just* like that, holding a book *just* like that.

"How about a story?" Grandpa turns back the bedspread, and I slip under it.

"Once upon a time there was a little boy called Michael Nidetzky, and he lived in America, in a little town in Ohio. It was the year 1857, and the boy was ten years old. His friends didn't call him Michael, they called him Thomas Alva Edison. No one knows how he got that nickname. . . ."

I know this story already. When I'm grown up—I mean when Thomas Alva is grown up, of course—I invent the phonograph, the carbon filament lamp, the cinematograph, the vitascope and all sorts of other very important things. Because I'm the greatest inventor of all time.

But today I don't feel I want to hear the story right through. Grandpa is hurt because I interrupt him.

"When do you have to go to the hospital, Grandpa?"

"Who, me?" Grandpa's train of thought is broken. "The day after tomorrow."

I ask if the examinations will hurt. A bit, he says. He should know, he had some once before, a year ago. Grandpa shakes his head. "Can't see any point in it, myself. The doctors aren't going to find out anything new, that's certain. Anyone can see with half an eye there's nothing to be done for me now."

If that's so, I don't understand why Grandpa is going.

"Hope, that's why. Hope's a funny thing. Sometimes you hope a miracle will happen. And it would be a miracle, if I were suddenly to get better again."

"But perhaps there really will be a miracle!" I cry. "I mean, there could be."

"No." Grandpa shakes his head. "I don't really believe in one. Perhaps that's my trouble. There are people who believe so firmly in miracles that they actually do happen. Have you ever heard of Lourdes?"

"Lour—what? No."

"It's a kind of shrine where pilgrims go, in the south of France. The Mother of God appeared there eighteen times, to a girl called Bernadette. Bernadette was made a saint later, I'm not sure just why. Anyway, there's a spring of water in Lourdes, which is said to work miracles. So a lot of people went on pilgrimages to this spring. And one day the first miracle happened. Some sick person—I forget if he was blind or crippled—he could see again. Or walk."

Grandpa tells this story as if he didn't believe

the miracles had really happened.

"Oh yes, I believe they happened all right," he tells me. "But I don't believe Bernadette worked them; she was dead by then. And a spring of water—do you think a sip of water could make a blind man see again?"

"Of course not," I say.

"There you are! But the miracles happened, all the same. It was the people's faith, that's all it was. If you believe in something firmly enough, it can really come true. The sick people at Lourdes did believe. They believed in St. Bernadette. And in God."

"Don't you believe in God?"

"No, Michael. I never had much time for the Church. So far as I'm concerned, there isn't any God. Sometimes I envy those who do believe in him."

Funny, I always thought all old people believed in God. I sometimes go to the children's service on Sundays, and when it's over, and the grownups' service is beginning, you can see there's almost no one going in but old ladies and a few old men.

"I wish you could believe firmly enough in something, Grandpa."

"Well, I do!" laughs Grandpa. "I believe you're going to grow into a fine man."

* * *

We've taken Grandpa to hospital. I wasn't allowed to go in, because children under fourteen aren't allowed to visit. Grandpa has threatened to haunt me, like a spirit, if I worry too much while he's away.

"I'll be back home in four days' time." Grandpa

waved to me from the balcony, and I sat down on the green wooden bench outside, and wished I were somewhere else, a long way off. I can't stand hospitals. The nurses always wake you when it's still dark outside, and they keep taking your temperature. I know, because I had my appendix taken out two years ago. But the worst part was Mom only being allowed to visit me every other day. Grandpa once slipped in on a day when there weren't any visiting hours, and brought me my teddy bear.

I could try that. Smuggle myself in to see Grandpa. In disguise, maybe? In striped pajamas—then the nurses would think I was a patient too.

But the children's wards are in a different building. Phooey.

* * *

Grandpa is home again. He looks dreadful: he's so pale. Linda says he looks like a ghost. I don't think that's funny.

They took samples from Grandpa. I don't know what that means.

Grandpa doesn't want to talk about the examination. But he says, with a groan, that yes, it did hurt. It hurt a lot.

He can only eat horrible things now, without any salt and pepper. He can't have roast meat either. Just a funny kind of bread roll with fatless cheese spread on it.

"Ridiculous, the whole thing," he grumbles when Mom gives him another of these rolls with the fatless spread. "What difference does it make if I die a few days

sooner or later?" But I can see that it does make a difference to him because he sticks strictly to his diet now.

Grandpa has lost weight. I don't think he liked it
when I burst into the bathroom after lunch today while
he was standing on the scales in his knee-length white
underpants. He got off the scale in a hurry, and pre-
tended he'd been going to comb his hair, but he wasn't
holding a comb.

"How much do you weigh?" I asked him.

"One hundred and thirty-five pounds," he muttered.
"It was a hundred and forty-two a month ago."

"Well, of course you'll lose weight if you eat so little.
You have to eat more, that's all. Once you're better
again. . . ."

I stop in the middle of my sentence, because I have
remembered that Grandpa will never be better again.

I can't believe it. I do try—I try hard to grasp it. To
believe that Grandpa is so sick no one can help him. But
it's no good. I can't believe it.

* * *

It's Ferdi's birthday, and he can't have a party at home,
so Mom said we could have one for him here. It was
nice of her to give herself all that extra work when she
didn't have to.

We're inviting five more people from our class. Fat
Walter, who's coming in his Boy Scout uniform; he's
very proud of it. And Regina, who sits behind me at
school.

Rudi, Peter and Gernot are coming too. I don't
like them very much, but it's Ferdi's birthday party,

so he can invite anyone he wants.

Mom says Ferdi must feel perfectly at home with us. He does, too. We help her whip the cream and put frankfurters in hot water. There's cocoa, too, in a big pot, with skin on the top. Yuk! I hate skin.

Walter and Regina are at the garden gate at three o'clock. The others' parents bring them, by car. They don't live right in Purkersdorf, like us, they come from farther away.

My sister has cleared out. "A kids' birthday party—humph!" she said, sniffing. She's probably at Gerd's house, cuddling and so on.

We play a lot of games, and then Grandpa comes out into the garden and sits down on the seat among the birch trees.

"This is my grandpa," I tell the others.

"The one who's got cancer," adds Ferdi. Then he's so horrified to hear it slip out that he clasps his hand over his mouth.

Grandpa just looks at him. "Don't worry, Ferdi," he says. "It's perfectly true, you weren't telling a lie."

All the same, Ferdi is upset. "I know it's not the sort of thing people should say," he stammers.

"Because it's none of their business!" says Grandpa, smiling. "But you see, I don't mind who knows. I don't mind if the whole world knows. Do you think one should be ashamed of illness?"

And then Grandpa tells us a story. A story with all six of us in it. I'm King Arthur, and the others are my knights of the Round Table. It's nice to see everyone listening so intently to Grandpa. I have sometimes wondered if I'm too old for this sort of story but if the others are listening then it must be all right.

"Your grandpa is great!" says Rudi afterward. "Mine can't tell nearly such good stories. He spends practically all his time going on and on about how things used to be much, much better in the old days, when he was a little boy."

I can't imagine my grandpa as a little boy. A real baby, sucking my great-grandmother's breasts. I try to think of Grandpa as a baby, but the nearest I can get is a tiny Grandpa with glasses and long white hair. A mini-Grandpa.

*   *   *

I have a wonderful book. It's called *The Treasure in the Silver Lake*, it's very exciting. Mom has just been in to say goodnight, because it's nine o'clock.

Last year Grandpa gave me a flashlight for my birthday, it comes in handy now. I like reading under the covers.

I have to go to the bathroom, and I creep along the hallway very quietly, so Mom won't hear. She thinks people should remember to go to the bathroom before they get into bed. I hear voices in the kitchen. One of them is Grandpa's. I'm surprised. I thought he was back in bed ages ago.

"We ought to get the job done now, though," Grandpa is saying. I hold my breath and listen at the door. "I would like to write it all down, Paul, and you must witness it."

"But Father, that's—I mean, there's still plenty of time for you to make a will. Maybe in a couple of years' time—" That's Mom. She laughs. It doesn't sound like a real laugh. It's the same way she laughs when people ask her how she is.

"No," Grandpa insists. "It must be done now. At once."

Mom must be standing by the cupboard because I hear her open a door and take something out.

"I'll make coffee, Paul," she says.

"Well, the house, that's all clear. I'd like to turn it over to you two in the next day or so, to avoid the taxes. Then there are the securities—" A rustling sound. "Here we are, Paul, here are the stock certificates. They come to term in 1983, don't sell them before. They belong to you and Erica now. It isn't much, only two hundred thousand Austrian schillings—"

"Not much?" Mom puts the coffee mugs down on the table rather noisily. "I know how hard you've saved all your life!"

"Yes, and the more fool me!" says Grandpa. "I should have spent it—I ought to have done some traveling, had a good time, enjoyed myself. . . ." He sighs. "Ah, well, too late now! Nothing I can do about that. At least I'd like you two to reap the benefit! Oh yes, and here's another savings-account book. I'll hand that over to you as well."

"But this one's in Michael's name," says Dad.

"Yes, I've been putting aside a thousand schillings a month so he will have a little nest egg when he comes of age."

I can hear a scraping sound; it's a chair being pushed back. Footsteps come closer. I shoot around the corner and back to my room.

Grandpa worked for forty years. Monday to Friday, eight to five. He told me so himself. And now, all of a sudden, we're to get the money he saved up?

I suppose I ought to be pleased, especially about the savings book. I have no idea how much money Grandpa has saved up for me—when I'm eighteen it will all be mine. I'm not sure that I want the money. I bet I could use it to buy myself something nice. Like a bike with several gears. Or a stereo cassette recorder with a pair of speakers. And some records. . . .

All the same, it doesn't seem fair for Grandpa to have to die so that we'll get some money.

* * *

The bell by the garden gate rings. It's the baroness standing outside, underneath a huge black umbrella.

I don't know if she's really a baroness, but that's what Grandpa always calls her.

She's wearing a black coat with a horrible fur collar. It has foxes' heads still hanging on it. I feel sorry for those foxes. I wouldn't like to be hung around anyone's neck after I'm dead.

"Can I see Herr Nidetzky? The elder Herr Nidetzky?" she asks. She's been here quite often, but I don't think she remembers my name.

"Good afternoon, baroness." I open the gate for her.

"You must be little. . . ."

"I'm Michael." I feel the corners of my mouth twitch, trying not to laugh. She looks odd, walking up to the house with tiny little steps and holding the wet umbrella away from her.

The baroness is an old friend of Grandpa's. She was once married to someone else who worked in his office. He was higher up in the firm than Grandpa, a head of department or something. "It was quite a little flirtation," Dad once told me, grinning broadly. He said the baroness and Grandpa were once in love—really in love.

I take the baroness to Grandpa's room, and she knocks three times.

Grandpa calls out, "Come in!" He's wearing his good black suit because this is Thursday, and the baroness visits him on every third Thursday in the month.

"Black-suit day today," Linda said at breakfast. That always annoys Grandpa. His black suit is very old, and the jacket is thin at the elbows, and now he's so thin the trousers flap around his thighs.

I stand in the doorway, watching the baroness unpack what she's brought. A whole apple tart. "Homemade," she says.

Grandpa has already made coffee. "Aren't you having any, Herr Nidetzky?" asks the baroness, when he pours out hers.

"No, it's my heart, you know." Grandpa smiles, rather embarrassed.

"Oh, I see," says the baroness, shoving a huge piece of apple tart into her mouth. "But you'll have a piece of my apple tart, won't you?"

"Maybe later," says Grandpa. "I've only just had lunch, Frau Liesegang." That's the baroness's last name.

I can see he'd like to change the subject. "Grandpa mustn't!" I interrupt, because I've noticed the way he's looking at that apple tart.

"All right, Michael, you can go and do your homework now," says Grandpa. "Don't you have any homework today?"

Okay, I get the idea—I'm being thrown out. I'm surprised, and a bit hurt too. After all, I meant well. I go off to see Linda to tell her about the funny way Grandpa's behaving.

"Well, of course he is! It's only natural," she says. "You can bet he's still in love with the baroness, so he's ashamed of being old and sick."

"In that case she's the only person who makes him feel ashamed of it."

"Mmm," says my sister, shrugging her shoulders and tapping away at her pocket calculator like mad.

"Why do they call each other Herr Nidetzky and Frau Liesegang, instead of using their Christian names, if they're in love?"

"People used to stick to last names. So as to keep up appearances in public."

"So as to do what?"

Linda stands up, walks to the door and holds it open for me. "So no one would notice," she says. "I've got work to do."

So no one would notice what? That they were in love? Well, once upon a time, maybe—but now? I mean, the baroness is a widow, and Grandpa doesn't have a wife any more either.

I would love to know what those two are talking about: Grandpa in his black suit, and that funny little old lady. . . . I struggle with my conscience for a bit, and then I go to Grandpa's door and listen at the keyhole.

Sure enough, he's calling the baroness Elvira now. They're talking about the old days. Silly old stuff—I mean, reminiscences and so on. Not very interesting.

All the same, I still don't understand about keeping up appearances in public. What's the point of it?

My sister's boy friend Gerd is in the kitchen. He's eating cookies, stuffing them into his mouth one after another. Mom is glad Gerd likes them. She thinks Linda will marry Gerd some day, though not till she's old enough. That's why Mom is always so nice. No one asks my opinion, but if they did . . . well, I'd rather not have Gerd in our family. Mom should hear the way he talks about her behind her back. "Linda's mother, that old bag," he calls her. She'd soon change her mind about him.

I make a huge bubble with my gum. It pops. I've already done my homework, Grandpa wants to be alone with his baroness, and I don't want to stay in the kitchen, not with Gerd there.

Then my sister comes in. That's about all we needed. Gerd and Linda together—it's almost too much to stand. The way they keep looking at each other—honestly, it's like a couple of sick moon-calves! People in love always look at each other that way. People in love are crazy.

If I had a bike, I could ride over and see Ferdi. Mom doesn't want me to have a bike for my birthday. She says it's too dangerous to let a child out in the streets with a bicycle because of all the traffic.

Ferdi comes around the corner, ringing his bell. Speak of the devil!

"Coming to the playground?"

I hope there won't be any other children there. A few weeks ago Hansi, who's in our class, came past the playground with his parents, and next day he told everyone at school that Ferdi and I were going down the babies' slide. I wouldn't like to go through that again.

In fact there isn't anyone but us in the playground.

The ground is still soft from the rain. I go down the slide first. I landed right in the mud! That would happen when I'm wearing a clean pair of jeans! The playground's no fun any more.

"Oh, rats!" Ferdi looks at me gloomily. He knows what my mom thinks of dirty trousers.

We go into the bathroom in the café. I take off my jeans and Ferdi tries to wash off the mud. I stand in the corner, shivering in my underpants. The harder Ferdi rubs, the bigger the muddy patches get.

"How's your grandpa?" asks Ferdi, rubbing the material against itself so hard I'm afraid he'll make holes in it.

"All right." What else can I say? I can't tell him how Grandpa really is. He almost never says he's in pain, though I know he is. He doesn't even grumble about not being able to eat the same food as us. But yesterday I did notice Grandpa staring at my goulash with his mouth open. He was good, though; he kept eating his soup. It looked so horrible, the mere sight of it took my appetite away.

I get back into my jeans. They're soaking wet, they stick to my legs, and the muddy patches are still there.

If Mom doesn't notice them she must be blind.

"Shall we go and see your grandpa? Maybe he'll tell us a story, same as he did on my birthday, remember?" Ferdi looks enthusiastic. "That was a terrific story! Honestly!"

"We can't. He's got a visitor."

I tell Ferdi about the baroness. He doesn't know why two people who were once in love would use each other's last names, either.

"I can't imagine it—your grandpa in love with someone! Do you think he actually kissed her?" Ferdi giggles.

"Don't laugh!" I feel angry with him. I mean, of course Grandpa must have kissed the baroness.

But in a way Ferdi is right. I can't really imagine it myself. Grandpa is just Grandpa—and I only know my grandpa on his own, not with a woman around him. My grandma died before I was born.

My jeans just won't dry, and I'm shivering. "Come on, let's go home."

Ferdi nods. "Okay." He spits out his chewing gum. He can spit much farther than I ever could.

*　*　*

"Perhaps you're not taking enough care of him? The poor old gentleman is as thin as a rake!"

There's a cup of coffee in front of the baroness, and a few cookies that Gerd left: not many.

Mom is sitting on the sofa, with a fixed smile on her face.

"My dear Frau Liesegang, I need hardly reproach myself with that!"

I smell a quarrel brewing. There's been a lot of that recently. Like wasps. Must be a nest somewhere.

"But—" begins the baroness. However, Mom won't let her go on.

"Please!" says Mom, in a warning voice. "Not in front of the child." Right after that she clasps her hands in horror and touches my wet, muddy jeans.

All right, all right—yes, in the playground, yes, of course I'm going to change at once, yes, I expect I'll catch a cold. Yes, yes, yes. Honestly, sometimes it's enough to drive a person crazy!

*   *   *

"Ah yes, Elvira," sighs Grandpa, searching among a mountain of old photographs. "That's Baron Liese-gang—and here, this is her." Grandpa holds the photograph well away from him and half-closes his eyes. "She was still young then. And beautiful!"

I wouldn't have recognized the baroness from that photograph. The woman in the picture doesn't look at all like the woman who was sitting in our living room eating up my favorite cookies.

Grandpa says he thinks the baroness is still very beautiful. My face must have shown him that I didn't agree with him entirely. "Well, tastes differ," he says, shaking his head. "She hasn't grown any more beautiful, I'll grant you that. None of us gets any more beautiful. Take a look at me!"

But I think my grandpa is beautiful.

He doesn't believe me. "Michael, you're laying it on far too thick!" He laughs.

He gets up from his desk, reaching for his stick. These days he needs it more than he used to.

He goes into the kitchen, and I trot along behind him.

In a minute I'm going to make myself a nice thick piece of bread and butter with plenty of salt on it.

*   *   *

I got an A on my arithmetic homework. I'll have to show it to Grandpa the minute I get back. Ferdi got a C, and he doesn't dare go home. His father thinks it's the end of the world if you get C in arithmetic. He expects Ferdi to get all A's. He'll put up with an occasional B, but not too many of them. Poor Ferdi!

Grandpa's been indulging in a weakness for photographs recently. He's sitting at his desk again, going through his pictures. There were two boxes filled with them, and he's emptied them on the top of the desk. He seems to be searching for a particular photograph. He's muttering to himself. I can't make out exactly what he's saying, only a few words. "But it must be . . . now where did I? . . . no, is it here? . . . dear me, what a nuisance . . . surely I can't have lost it. . . ."

"Hello?" Grandpa didn't notice me when I came into his room, and now he jumps when he sees me, as if I'd appeared out of thin air.

"I got an A!" I tell him proudly, showing him my notebook.

"Good, good," he says. I'm disappointed that he doesn't look at it more closely. Today he just takes a quick look at the big red A and then gives me back my notebook.

He notices my puzzled look. "I'm trying to find a photograph," he explains.

Yes, I can see he's trying to find a photograph. "Which one?"

"A picture of Willi Jedlicka. Poor old Willi...." Grandpa's voice sounds sad. "He was just two years younger than me."

For the first time I see the white card with its black border and big black letters. It's a card to say someone has died.

"A dear husband, father, grandfather and uncle, suddenly and unexpectedly called to rest in his seventy-eighth year."

There are a whole lot of names underneath, and the date of the interment.

"What's an interment?" I ask, baffled. "Is it when they bury a dead person, lying on his back? Or do they bury people sitting up?" I can't remember which I thought it was.

"Lot of nonsense! An interment is the same as an ordinary funeral," says Grandpa. "This kind of high-flown language makes me mad!"

He hits the desk top with the palm of his hand. A couple of photos jump into the air as if they'd taken fright.

"Tell me truthfully, Michael, don't you sometimes think people are silly?" Grandpa is getting worked up. "Saying interment instead of funeral. Called to rest instead of died...."

"Departed this life," I think of another one.

"Fallen asleep, gone home. The Lord has taken him to Himself. . . ."

"He bit the dust!" I shout. That's what they say in the Westerns on TV. "He's pushing up daisies. . . ."

Grandpa knows some more, too. "Pegged out. Kicked the bucket. His last hour has struck—no one actually likes to say someone's died, these days. Just plain died. He's dead. Dead as a doornail. Full stop."

"I think the one about pushing up the daisies is the funniest."

"Hm. I'm not so sure." Grandpa shakes his head doubtfully. "Imagine someone lying in a coffin covered with daisies, trying to push them up while the priest is delivering a sermon—no, it's not solemn enough!" Grandpa chuckles to himself. "Well, you've really cheered me up, Michael. I'm glad you came. I was feeling quite depressed—poor old Willi Jedlicka. We began our training at Reichert's together, Willi and I. That was in 1912—or was it '13? Before the war, anyway. I wonder what Willi died of?"

Grandpa is speaking quietly now, as if I weren't here at all, as if he were just talking to himself.

"Would it have been a stroke? He always looked quite a bit younger than me. Sound as a bell, too. . . ."

"What exactly does a stroke mean? Did something strike him?"

I never really thought about it before. Grandpa laughs; I don't know why.

"Silly boy, no, what an idea! I mean, he could have had a heart attack or something of that kind, when someone's heart simply stops beating. That's the best kind of death."

"Why?" I don't get it.

"Because it's the quickest. You don't feel much."

He says Willi is being buried the day after tomorrow. "You can come with me if you like," says Grandpa.

I think he means it to be a treat for me. I'm not all that eager. I don't like cemeteries. Scary things go on there, especially at midnight.

And what's more, Mom is sure to want me to wear my black suit, the one with its sleeves too short for me, and I can't button the middle button any more.

* * *

"Put your black suit on!" says Mom.

I've grown again. I have to wear black socks, otherwise everyone could see the trousers are far too short. And I have to wear a tie too. Mom helps me put it on. I don't like having her fuss over me all the time, and I'm glad when the taxi finally draws up at our garden gate.

Mom insisted that we must have a taxi. At first Grandpa didn't want one, but once we're inside it he's glad. "I'm not as fit as I was a year ago," he admits. I'm sure he'd never have said that if Mom were here.

Grandpa is watching the meter anxiously, and he asks the driver how much the journey will cost. The driver grunts in an unfriendly way, and Grandpa tells me in a whisper that taxi drivers are dishonest, getting rich at the expense of the man in the street. He whispers a bit too loud.

"You want to get out, mister?" asks the taxi driver. "Because if not, you might keep your mouth shut!"

Grandpa is angry, but he doesn't want to get out so

he keeps his mouth shut. He goes on staring at the meter, as if fascinated.

He pays two hundred schillings without even a protest, but he doesn't give the driver a tip.

"It's worth the money, for Willi," murmurs Grandpa, but I can tell he hates handing over so much money.

Mom says Grandpa is a miser, but that's not true, he's just frugal.

The Central Cemetery is enormous, and there are thousands of graves there. I think there'd be too many for me to count even if I had a whole week to do it.

I've been here once before, when we came to decorate Aunt Resi's grave and light candles in the little lantern on it. I didn't know Aunt Resi. She wasn't a real aunt either.

Grandpa says we must hurry. It's nearly two-thirty, and Grandpa doesn't like arriving late. He knows his way around the cemetery because a lot of his school friends are buried here.

Grandpa stops, panting for breath, though we've been walking very slowly and haven't gone very far.

"There!" Grandpa points his stick at the building ahead of us. "That's where we're going; it's the funeral parlor."

He walks slowly on.

"And be quiet," he adds.

"Yes, okay." A real load of fun, this is! I kick up a few pebbles.

There are two ladies walking ahead of us. Grandpa says good afternooon to them. They all used to work in the same office.

"You're not looking too good," I hear one of these

67

ladies tell Grandpa. I'm drawing little men in the gravel with my foot, and I'm bored stiff. I wish I were back at home.

"First class or second class?"

For a moment I think the lady is talking about me, and I'm about to open my mouth and say no, I'm in the fourth class now, when I realize she doesn't mean me at all.

Grandfather explains, before we go into the funeral parlor. Apparently there are different sorts of funeral. A first-class funeral costs much more than a second-class funeral—and for very poor people, there's a poor person's funeral which is free.

"Idiotic, isn't it?" says Grandpa crossly, and I don't think he minds that the ladies can hear him perfectly. "And they say all men are equal in the sight of God! There's no equality, even in death!" Grandpa is talking louder and louder. "The poor people don't get any music at the graveside, just a few pious words from the priest, and that's it. But if it's a first-class funeral, the priest preaches for hours on end, and there's a choir singing, at wicked expense, with full orchestra. . . ."

"Herr Nidetzky! Please don't blaspheme like that!" hisses the lady on Grandpa's left. "Suppose one of the family heard you?"

"Well?" Grandpa goes on talking. When he's in full swing he's not likely to stop in a hurry. "At home, the dead person's relatives may be living on bread and water because they can't afford anything better, but of course there has to be an alabaster coffin for the corpse, on account of the neighbors. So they'll think the family is prosperous!"

"Herr Nidetzky, please!"

"Yes, yes, all right! It's true, though! And they call themselves Christians. Do *you* believe in God?"

"Who—me?" The lady looks very confused.

"All good Christians here, eh?" Grandpa goes on grumbling. "Don't worry, ma'am, I've nothing against God if He exists. But I wonder, can you tell me why all these people here are crying if the dead man is really going to God? It's supposed to be a delightful prospect! Crying because someone has died—why, they should be singing and dancing for joy to think of a good Christian going to heaven!"

"For goodness sake, it's usual—after all, one does feel sad—Herr Nidetzky, you are still being blasphemous!"

A few people have noticed this going on. Grandpa is red in the face, and I'm shifting from foot to foot.

"Ssh." The lady points to a group which has just come in. The Jedlicka family. It's three o'clock. We were half an hour early.

I've been busy listening to Grandpa, but now I see there's a coffin in the middle of the room. I'm disappointed because the lid is closed. Grandpa said you can sometimes look into the coffin and see the corpse; corpses wear makeup and have pink cheeks, and he says they look more lifelike than when they were really alive.

The lid stays closed. An organ begins to play; it's like being in church. There's a priest here too, a Catholic one, and when the organ stops playing the priest sprinkles water on the coffin. Not ordinary tap water, holy water. There are two boys not much older than me standing behind the priest. They're his acolytes.

The priest says the Lord's Prayer, and the Hail Mary,

and a few people mutter the words with him, but either they don't know the prayers, or they aren't sure if joining in is allowed.

Grandpa tries to grab my hand and hang on to me, but I worm my way through to the front. I don't like having so many grownups blocking my view.

There are wreaths leaning up against the wall, big wreaths and little ones, with black bows and gold writing on them.

"In loving memory, from your children who. . . ." I can't read the rest of it, because the bow is partly hidden behind another wreath, a smaller one which says it's from the Goal Soccer Club.

Suddenly, as if they'd risen out of the ground, there are four men standing by the coffin, two on each side. They're the bearers. They look like generals, with black uniforms and silver braids and epaulettes. They have hats like Napoleon's, only worn the wrong way round, with the two points at the front and back of their heads.

The bearers carefully lift the coffin on to their shoulders and walk slowly away.

There's a crush. I'm afraid I might lose Grandpa. "Grandpa!" I call.

"Ssh!" hisses a man in black beside me. But Grandpa has spotted me.

We wait until the room is almost empty. The other people are outside now, following the coffin in a long procession.

It's begun to rain, only a few drops at first, but harder now.

One of the acolytes walks at the very front, holding a cross up in the air. It reminds me of a film I once saw on

TV. I can still remember its name—it was called *Dance of the Vampires*, and they kept on holding up crosses in this film to get rid of vampires.

"Are there any vampires here?" I ask Grandpa in a whisper.

"Yes, and vultures too," he whispers back. "All the people who make money out of death. The cemetery gardener, and the gravedigger, and the layer-out of the corpse, and the stonemason. The firm who printed the card with the funeral announcement, and the undertakers. The carpenter who made the coffin, the priest. . . ."

"No, I mean real vampires. You know—with teeth." And I tell Grandpa why I thought of them.

"What ideas you get in your head!" Grandpa smiles, and holds my hand tight.

The priest is walking behind the acolyte. Sometimes he looks up at the sky, as if that would make the rain stop sooner. One of the acolytes runs off, probably to get an umbrella.

The four generals walk behind the priest, pushing a cart with the coffin on it. They all look as sad as our school caretaker's spaniel.

Next comes the family, then the people who knew the dead man *very* well, then the people who knew him *well.* . . .

"And finally the people who knew him *slightly,*" says Grandpa.

"Like you?"

"That's it. Like me."

And like the two ladies from Grandpa's office, who are walking behind us. We go on and on and on, it looks as though we'll never stop. Past thousands of gravestones, or that's how it feels to me.

Some of them are beautiful, especially the old ones, where you can hardly read the inscriptions because the stone is so weatherbeaten. They have marble doves perching beside fat-cheeked little angels with their wing tips missing.

There are some little gravestones too, with children buried under them. Sometimes round frames have been cut into the stones. Photographs of children have been put in them: old, sepia photographs like some of the ones in Grandpa's boxes. The new, modern gravestones aren't as nice. They're all the same height and the same width, and the only difference between them is their inscriptions.

We're still walking. My feet hurt, and Grandpa must be worn out; he's leaning heavily on his stick.

I almost collided with the man in front of me just now, because the procession of mourners came to a sudden stop. The coffin is standing on a frame above the open grave.

The woman right at the front, the one with a black veil over her face, is crying. I think she's quite old, though you can't see for sure through the veil. "That's the dead man's wife," whispers Grandpa. "Only she isn't his wife any more, she's his widow now."

The priest is talking again. There's no bench anywhere in sight where Grandpa could sit down. "I could perch on a gravestone," suggests Grandpa quietly, "but that sort of thing isn't done."

The priest is telling us not to be sad because the dear departed has left us.

"You see?" I tell Grandpa, because of what he was

saying earlier about Christians liking to be sad.

"Ssh!" says Grandpa, and the man in front turns around and frowns at me.

Some people are crying. I can't see anything, and I don't like all this. I don't know why.

Grandpa coughs. He takes his handkerchief out of his coat pocket and blows his nose. I realize he's crying a bit, too. Not much, but he is crying.

Grandpa looks sideways at me. I'm on his right. "I'm an old fool," he says, trying to grin, but he doesn't manage too well.

"Sheer sentimentality," he whispers.

I don't know what he means. I decide to ask him later.

The priest sprinkles the coffin with more holy water, and the bearers let it down into the grave. It's only hanging from a couple of linen bands now. I wish it would tip over and fall in. I think that would be funny. Then it wouldn't be so quiet here, and maybe some of the people would laugh. . . . Sometimes my ideas frighten me.

There's a gravedigger beside the grave, looking just as bored as I feel. He's holding a bowl full of earth, with a little toy shovel in the middle. The priest scoops up a bit of earth with the shovel and throws it into the grave, on top of the coffin. It goes plop; it's a weird sound.

One by one, people go up to the grave and throw earth into it. Grandpa goes too. Plop . . . plop . . . I follow him, and suddenly I'm standing on the wooden plank by the graveside. The priest smiles, and the gravedigger puts the little shovel in my hand. I'm afraid to look down at the grave, I might fall in. My bit of earth goes plop too, and I jump off the plank in a hurry, almost falling flat on my face!

I look around for Grandpa. He's standing at the end of a line, and he holds out his hand. "I must offer my condolences," he says. "That's like offering congratulations, only the other way round. You shake hands with the dead person's family and say how sorry you are. 'My heartfelt sympathy,' or, 'We shall never forget him.'"

But Grandpa himself doesn't say anything, he just shakes the widow's hand and walks away. I shake her hand too, and say, "Good afternoon." That just slips out automatically. I don't think it was the right thing to say, because several people are frowning at me.

"There, that's it," says Grandpa. "Now they all go off to a funeral party and stuff themselves with food."

"Us too?" I ask hopefully.

No, not us. It's only for the family and the first-class friends, Grandpa explains. And I'm so hungry, too.

Grandpa promises me we'll stop at a sausage stand and I can buy a hot sausage.

"Well, what did you think of it, Michael?" Grandpa asks, when we're in a taxi and I'm eating my sausage.

"Boring," I say, honestly. "Dead boring."

*   *   *

I'm lying on the carpet listening to the new Abba record. Ferdi lent it to me. Frau Novotny shouts at me to turn the volume down. There's a smell of baking. Mom and Frau Novotny are making cookies for Christmas, and they've chased me out of the kitchen twice already. I like the batter better than the cookies, but Mom doesn't like me running my finger around the bowl. And Frau Novotny says the batter gives you a stomachache. Her daughter, who's gone to live in America, ate some batter when she was a child and she got such bad pains she had to be taken to the hospital in an ambulance. I don't believe a word Frau Novotny says.

It's raining outside. I hope it will snow soon, and then Ferdi and I can build our ski jump on the little hill out in the garden again.

Dr. Gnad's blue Peugeot drives up. I run down to open the gate for the doctor, because he doesn't have an umbrella with him. He goes right in to see Grandpa. Grandpa is having an injection every other day now, so that he won't feel so much pain.

The doctor was angry with Grandpa for going to Willi Jedlicka's funeral. I heard him telling Mom that something like that was too much of a strain for Grandpa. And Frau Novotny was standing in the doorway of the kitchen, wiping her hands on her apron and nodding. A nod every few seconds or so.

Grandpa's eyes are closed.

"Shall I make you a cup of tea, Grandpa?" Grandpa can't drink coffee now, only camomile tea with artificial sweetener.

"Yes, please." Grandpa runs his tongue over his lips. They're split; all dry and rough. He must be tired.

In fact, he's so tired that he asks me to come back in an hour's time, because he says he'd like to sleep now.

He does look better after an hour's sleep. He asks me to read him something out of the newspaper. He's mislaid his glasses, and I look all over the room for them, but I can't find them anywhere.

I read to Grandpa for quite a long time. First the headlines on the front page, then the sports reports, and the bit about where you can buy beef cheapest this week. I was going to leave out the small ads, but Grandpa wants them too. Even the deaths column.

"Frau Elise Grabowski. Born January 18, 1908," I read.

"Only seventy-two." Grandpa is pleased. "She was younger than me!"

I give him his camomile tea. He's very thirsty.

"Soon the apple tree will be blossoming, Michael," he tells me.

"Not in the middle of winter!" Grandpa does get some odd ideas.

"Only a joke. If an apple tree blossoms at the end of autumn, it means someone will soon die."

"That's not true, is it?"

"No, just an old superstition. I suddenly remembered it."

And Grandpa tells me that some people think it means a death in the family if a hen crows like a cock. Or if a tree suddenly dries up, or a mirror or glass breaks, if the light flickers or a clock ticks in a funny way or stops. If a door opens all by itself, or there's a moaning sound in the house and you don't find someone doing it just to play a trick—they're all sure signs of the death of someone you know well.

I feel a cold shudder run down my spine.

"And of course, you must never have three lights burning in a room all at the same time," Grandpa tells me. I hastily count the lights. Thank goodness, there are four turned on. It's all nonsense, I know that, but I'm relieved.

"People can be so superstitious, can't they?" Grandpa didn't notice how scared I felt.

"Don't worry, Michael," he adds. "You can put one of the lights out. I'll be dying anyway!"

And Grandpa laughs. He laughs! I can't understand that—I mean, if I knew I'd be dying soon, I couldn't laugh. Or could I? I think it's fantastic that Grandpa can still be so cheerful.

*   *   *

It's my birthday—and the sun is shining. It's been raining for two weeks, but today, my birthday, the sky is bright blue.

Linda has come into my room, and she's standing there singing "Happy Birthday to You," with Mom behind her, smiling and standing arm in arm with Dad, so that Frau Novotny can't see past them and look at my birthday presents.

I got a bike after all. A brand new one. And five books, and a very nice dark blue suit.

My sister gave me a new paintbox, and Frau Novotny knitted me a cap and scarf in lovely bright colors. That was nice of her.

There's cocoa with whipped cream for breakfast, the same as always on my birthday. I have to go to school, though. Too bad this isn't a Sunday.

I'm so excited I forget to go and say good morning to Grandpa.

"What do you know?" I tell Ferdi, at school. "I forgot Grandpa."

Ferdi doesn't think that was so awful, but I feel bad about it. I don't like myself at all. I'm sure Grandpa was waiting to wish me a happy birthday. I buy him some flowers on the way home. It takes all my pocket money.

I didn't need to feel bad about it. When I try going to Grandpa's room, my sister stops me.

"Grandpa's still asleep."

Linda tells me Mom called the doctor in the middle of the night. Grandpa was in such pain that he needed an injection, only no one told me because it's my birthday.

Grandpa doesn't wake up till four in the afternoon.

"Hello, Michael, how's the birthday boy?" he asks weakly. His face twists.

"Are you in pain again, Father?" Mom pulls the covers up to Grandpa's chin. He growls and pushes them back again.

"Far too hot in here."

I throw the window open, and put another cup of camomile tea into Grandpa's hand. He reaches for the yellow tablets Dr. Gnad prescribed for him, and swallows some.

"Ugh!" Grandpa shakes himself.

"Poor Grandpa."

"Nonsense!" he grunts. "I'm all right." He tries to smile, but it turns into a wry sort of grin. "Well, it does hurt," he finally admits. Then he says, quickly, "I wasn't able to get out and buy you a birthday present, Michael."

"It doesn't matter," I tell him. What a pity. I was

sure Grandpa would give me something.

"So you can choose what you like out of my treasure chest."

That's great! The treasure chest is Grandpa's oldest collection, the one that's kept up in the attic. I run upstairs and haul it out from among the old trunks and the broken piano.

I know just what I'm looking for: the magnifying glass with the ivory handle. I've wanted it for ages. Usually, Grandpa won't let me explore his treasure chest if he isn't there, but I can't help but look at it when I go up to the attic with Mom or Frau Novotny to help hang up the wash—I always look at it.

Everything's different, seen through the magnifying glass. I go close up to Grandpa with it. Suddenly he has a huge great eye—it looks weird. And his nostrils are like deep caves. It is spooky!

Grandpa makes a funny sound, presses his lips tightly together and puts both hands to his stomach. His stomach has grown bigger and bigger over the last few weeks, though he hardly eats anything at all. But his arms and legs are getting thinner all the time, and so is his face.

"Does it hurt very much, Grandpa?"

Grandpa nods, and one corner of his mouth turns down. He pats the pillow and raises his head and shoulders. I take the pillow away so he can lie flat, the way he likes to.

"Shall I get Mom?" I ask, and Grandpa nods again. Mom phones the doctor. He arrives half an hour later, and Grandpa is given an injection and gets very, very quiet.

Dad has just come home. I heard the door shut behind him.

"Is it very bad?" he asks the doctor anxiously.

Dr. Gnad is putting his coat on. "Well, he's in severe pain," he says.

"And how long. . . ." Dad doesn't go on.

"Dad wants to know how much longer Grandpa will live," I say, to help him out.

Mom takes a deep breath and looks at me angrily. "The things that boy says!" she says apologetically to Dr. Gnad. "I just don't know where he—"

The doctor shakes his head. He wasn't listening to Mom at all. "It's hard to tell," he says to Dad and me. "A month, maybe two. Maybe only two weeks. . . ."

*　*　*

Two weeks. That's ridiculous. That can't be true! It won't even be Christmas in two weeks. Two weeks—it's very soon. We're going for a school visit to the Natural History Museum in two weeks, exactly two weeks today.

"Michael, stop daydreaming and eat!"

My soup is cold.

"Can I have Grandpa's room when he's dead?"

"Linda!" Dad looks angrily at my sister.

Mom jumps up, runs round the table and slaps Linda once on each cheek.

"There!" says Mom, sitting down again. She puts her face in her hands and starts to cry.

Linda doesn't make a sound. She doesn't utter a word, she doesn't even cry, but there are two large red patches on her cheeks.

I drink my cold soup as fast as I can.

Dad is angry with Mom. He says she shouldn't have slapped Linda for saying a thing like that. I pull at Linda's sweater. My sister stands up, and I follow her to the door. No one stops us. We go to Linda's room.

"That was rotten of Mom!" cries Linda. She's in a rage the moment the door is closed; she throws herself on her bed. And now she's crying. I look at her book of horror stories while I wait for her to stop.

"Can you imagine Grandpa being gone, all of a sudden?" I ask when she's finished. "I mean, really dead—not here at all any more?"

Linda stares at me. She shrugs her shoulders. "I don't know—sometimes I can, sometimes I can't—oh, how should I know?" She thinks. "Everybody has to die some time. And Grandpa is old." Then she yawns. "And we can't think up anything to stop people dying. You'd better go to bed, Michael. "

"Well, I bet you don't get Grandpa's room!" I say, turning around and going out. I can feel her staring at me. I expect her mouth is still open. I wanted to hurt her.

* * *

"No," says Mom, standing outside the doorway. "You can't go in now."

I can't understand why she won't let me see Grandpa. I don't want to bother him, just sit by his bed for a few minutes.

"No, Michael. No!"

I'm so furious I don't know what to do! When Dad comes home, he'll tell her a thing or two!

Mom sends me off to do my homework. Then she disappears into Grandpa's room again. "Frau Novotny, just take a look at Michael's homework will you?" she calls, in the direction of the kitchen. That really is the end.

When you're feeling so angry, you can't possibly concentrate, certainly not on a composition about "My Ideal Christmas Vacation."

The minute Dad is through the front door I run up to him, complaining about Mom at the top of my voice.

"He's *my* grandpa," I cry, "and he's only Mom's father-in-law!"

Dad says I'm being silly, and to calm down. He promises to speak to Mom. "She means it for the best, Michael, she doesn't want you to see Grandpa suffering."

"I don't care about that," I say, trying not to cry.

I write my composition as fast as I can. I won't get anything better than a C—it's only after I've written the last line that I realize I've probably got the subject wrong. I wrote a description about the way we spent last Christmas.

Doesn't matter.

Dad comes to get me from my room. "Come along," he says, leading me into Grandpa's room.

Grandpa's eyes are half open, half closed. He raises his hand a little way, and tries to say something, but though his lips move, no words come out.

"It's the injections," Dad murmurs. Grandpa really

does look sick now. His face is thin and pale, with drops of sweat gleaming on his forehead.

"Grandpa!" I put my hand on his arm. Grandpa opens his eyes, but only for a moment, then they close again.

Dad signals to me to go out. Frau Novotny is standing outside the door, blowing her nose.

"Oh dear, poor Herr Nidetzky, oh, how dreadful!" she says shakily, and suddenly I feel sorry for her.

"It's only the injections," I tell her. "That's what makes Grandpa so tired."

* * *

"Grandpa is dead!"

Linda is shaking me. I haven't even got my eyes open yet.

"Michael, Grandpa has died."

I bolt upright in bed. Something constricts, right inside me. I jump out and put my slippers on.

"Now what?" I ask, not expecting any answer. I don't know what to do.

My sister is staring out of the window. It's still dark outside.

The door of Grandpa's room is not quite closed; I can hear quiet voices. I push it a little farther open with my foot. Mom has her back to me; she's standing by Grandpa's bed. Dad is sitting in the old leather armchair, staring at the picture above the bed.

Suddenly he stands up, comes to the door and opens it wide. I face Dad. He puts his arm round my shoulders, squeezing my arm so hard it hurts.

Grandpa is lying there in bed—the same as ever, really. He's asleep. No, he isn't asleep. Linda said Grandpa was dead.

Or is he asleep after all? That's what it looks like. And it looks as if he were smiling very slightly in his sleep. His arms are outside the covers.

Mom jumps when she sees me. Dad puts his finger gently on her lips.

"Grandpa doesn't feel any more pain now, Michael," says Dad.

"No," I say. "No."

He's right. I didn't think of that before. Perhaps it's better for Grandpa, being dead instead of in pain all the time. In fact I'm sure it is.

Suddenly I feel cheerful.

"Then Grandpa's all right now!" I say out loud, rather surprised.

Mom sobs. "Yes. I hope so—now that he has gone to rest."

"Grandpa doesn't like people saying silly things like that," I protest. "He told me so, in the cemetery. Grandpa is *dead*. He simply *died!*"

But Mom wasn't listening to me. I wait for her to say something, but she just goes on crying quietly.

I can't stop looking at Grandpa. He simply died.

It was all so quick. Yesterday he was still breathing. Today he doesn't move any more. My grandpa is dead.

* * *

Ignatius goes racing round his wheel as if nothing had happened. I would like to be a hamster. Nothing but eating and sleeping and running. . . .

"It's best for him to go to school. What would he do, hanging around the house?"

They're talking about me. What on earth is Mom's idea? I'd be at least half an hour late. What am I supposed to tell Herr Mühlhuber? My grandpa died last night? Well, why not? It's true.

I put my arithmetic book in my book bag.

Dr. Gnad has just been here. Dad says he has to make out a death certificate. The doctor writes down what the patient died of on this certificate, and then everything's in order.

All right, I will go to school! Frau Novotny is all upset too, using up lots of handkerchiefs. Mom's eyes are swollen, and Dad looks dreadful. Linda has disappeared; she'll be down at the bus stop by now, for sure.

"I'm sure Grandpa doesn't want you to cry," I say.

"How would you know?" sobs Frau Novotny.

"Michael is perfectly right," says Dr. Gnad.

* * *

"Sorry," I say breathlessly, "but my grandpa's just died."

Herr Mühlhuber is taken aback, and some of the children laugh.

"There's nothing to laugh about," Herr Mühlhuber tells them sternly.

"Really and truly?" Ferdi whispers to me.

He wants to hear all about it. How Grandpa looks now, whether dying hurt him, when he's going to be buried. . . .

I don't know that, either. I should have stayed at home. Maybe Grandpa won't be there when I get back from school.

"Are you sure he's really dead?" asks Ferdi. "Absolutely certain he isn't breathing any more?"

And he tells me how dead people in films—not real dead people, I mean actors playing the parts of dead people—have a board underneath their shirts so you won't see them breathing in close-ups.

But Ferdi doesn't think Grandpa would have had a board over his chest.

* * *

Mom is breaking eggs into the frying pan.

"We must make do with a quick snack today. Want a glass of milk with it?"

I cut myself another slice of bread. The bell by the garden gate rings.

"Oh, good heavens—they've come to lay him out!" cries Mom. "I don't know if I'm coming or going!" She hurries to open the gate.

There are two people, a man and a woman. They walk past the kitchen.

Then I hear the door of Grandpa's room open.

What are they doing to my grandpa?

"I wouldn't like to be watching," says Frau Novotny. "I did once—at my neighbor's. They're rough when they lay out the corpse; what do they care about cracking a bone or two?"

A piece of fried egg sticks in my throat. I know exactly why I don't like Frau Novotny—it's because she

86

always says the wrong thing at the wrong time.

Mom is pale when she comes back to the kitchen.

"Don't you have any homework to do today?" she asks me. And when I say I do she sends me straight to my room.

The bell rings again. I look out of the window and see a black limousine outside the garden gate. There's a coffin being carried into the house. A dark brown coffin. Is Grandpa getting first class or second class?

After a while the coffin is carried out to the car again. And I know my grandpa is inside it.

"So long, Grandpa," I say. But very softly, so that no one can hear me.

* * *

I have to wear the suit I got for my birthday. Mom has borrowed a black coat and skirt from a friend, and Dad has had a black suit made especially for the funeral. He says he needed a new one anyway, so he's killing two birds with one stone.

My sister has been crying her eyes out, but not because she's sad. It's on account of her fight with Mom. Linda doesn't want to wear a skirt, she wants to wear her black pants instead. Mom thinks that's disrespectful. So she said.

Grandpa has been dead two days now. But in a way he's still here—and I don't know quite how to explain that. Perhaps it's because everyone's been talking about him these last two days. I can't imagine it will ever be any different.

Our family are buried in the Baumgartner Cemetery.

My grandma is buried there already, and Grandpa is going to be buried in the same grave, on top of Grandma's coffin.

This time I'm standing right at the front of the funeral parlor. This time I'm one of the people walking at the head of the procession, just behind the coffin.

The cart with the coffin on it sways a little. Don't fall off, Grandpa, I think, and at the same time I realize falling off wouldn't make any difference to him. He wouldn't get bruises now, and it can't hurt him either.

It's all like Willi Jedlicka's funeral. Only Grandpa isn't there beside me today.

They lower the coffin down into the grave, the priest throws a little earth on it, then Mom and then Dad.

I feel fine, because I know all about this. I feel more experienced than the rest of them. I don't cry, because I don't need to.

"Michael!" whispers Dad, tugging my sleeve. "Your turn!" I stand on a wooden plank, someone puts the little shovel into my hand, but I can't throw the earth. The coffin is so far down. I can't throw earth on my grandpa! I feel sick! I'm getting dizzy. Everything is turning around and around. . . .

*   *   *

". . . and then he shouted, 'Grandpa!' and fell down. Fainted, poor boy!"

The voice is a long way off. I don't know whose it is. I'm lying on the back seat of a car. Our car.

"Michael. . . ." A large face looms over me. My sister smiles at me.

"Hello." That's my own voice. "What happened?"
"You fainted," she explains.

My head is buzzing. I feel tired, very tired. Hot, too.

"It's all over, Michael." Dad gives me a pat, then he gets behind the steering wheel. My sister puts my head on her lap. We drive away.

I close my eyes.

* * *

"Well, your temperature's going down." Mom takes the thermometer out of my mouth. "Nearly normal now."

I still feel weak. Mom says I must stay in bed, and I have to drink milk with honey in it.

It's nice in bed. I wish I didn't ever have to get up again. And I'd like to have Mom go on spoiling me. I pester her to say she'll read aloud to me.

I give a groan. Mom is worried, but I'm really all right. I just wanted to know if it sounded genuine.

I'd like to hear a story now. A good story. A Michael Nidetzky story.

"A what story?" asks Mom, puzzled.

Once upon a time there was a little boy, and his name was Michael Nidetzky. One day his grandpa died, and he was all alone in the world. . . .

I can hear Grandpa's voice. . . . But he isn't really here.

All the same, I know just how it sounded.

And now I can't help crying. I'm feeling sorry for

myself! It's silly! But the tears keep coming all by themselves!

* * *

"Hi, pal!" Ferdi is sitting on my bed, swinging his legs.
The mattress bounces in time to them. "You've been
lazing around long enough."

I'm glad to see Ferdi. "I'm sick!" I wail.

"No, you aren't," Ferdi tells me. "Your mom said you
don't have any temperature today."

That's true. I've slept the whole night and half the
day, without noticing.

Oh, it's too bad! As soon as I wake up I can't help
thinking of Grandpa, and then the tears come back.

"Are you nuts?" Ferdi pinches my cheek. "You're not
crying about your grandpa, are you?"

I swallow.

"I feel so sad!" I'm crying again. I can't help it.

Then Ferdi shouts at me; he's really mad. The thing
is, I told him about Willi Jedlicka's funeral, and the
things Grandpa said to me then.

"And now you're lying in bed crying and feeling
sorry for yourself!"

He's right, too.

"Got that Abba record here?" I ask. Ferdi carries it
with him all the time.

He puts it on. I crawl out of bed and turn the volume up.

"Quiet!" shouts Mom, but today I don't care. I turn
the key in my door, and Ferdi and I sing the songs along
with the record, as loud as we can.

* * *

"What nerve!" Dad is frowning. "Like a vulture."

"Poor Father not cold in his grave before she turns up!" Mom agrees with him.

The vulture is the baroness. She came to the funeral too—and today she came to ask if "the late Herr Nidetzky" had left her anything. She said he'd promised her a savings account book.

Dad was very angry, and nearly threw her out, but he didn't have to, she left when she realized there wasn't anything for her to inherit.

Now Dad is watching her leave. I feel sorry for her. Such a funny little old lady. Perhaps she really did love Grandpa once.

Linda is setting the table, and Dad is adjusting the seasoning of the spaghetti sauce. He's very proud of his spaghetti sauce; it's the one thing he can cook well.

After supper, Dad puts a letter into my hand.

"It's for you," he says. "Aren't you going to open it?"

Dad is curious. I can tell he'd love to know what it says.

The letter is from Grandpa. I know his writing very well. Beautiful, stylish handwriting, the sort I'm certainly never going to have. I read the letter out loud.

Dear Michael,

I hope you have not cried too much, and are not sad now. There's nothing to be sad about, you see, so just remember that!

I know that you are very much like me, and so that is why I want you, and nobody else, to have my "treasures." You know what I mean. The binoculars and the inkwells, the microscopes

91

and the box of glasses. You are to have the treasure chest too, but I think you had better keep it for your children and add new treasures now and then.

The books are for you as well; your parents must keep them for you, and when you are older you can decide which you want to keep and which you don't.

Don't forget the Michael Nidetzky stories. I would have liked to tell you more of them.

And there is something I wish for you; I hope your life will be just as happy as mine has been.

With love and kisses,
Grandpa

I feel happy. It's the nicest letter I have ever had. Mom has tears in her eyes. I wish she didn't.

"Stop crying, Mom," I say firmly. "There's nothing to be sad about, you see, so just remember that!"

And Mom tries to smile.

"Will I get Grandpa's room, though, all the same?" asks Linda anxiously.

Dad says that was decided long ago. My sister's mind is set at rest.

I go into Grandpa's room, sit on his bed and swing my legs. I feel them touch something hard. It's the bowl of pickled eggs. I wonder where it will be next year. . . .

I put the box of glasses on the bed and try them all on one by one.

And suddenly all the sadness has gone away. Sadness over Grandpa's being dead. Because he isn't really dead, not as long as someone is still thinking of him.

And I promise myself I will never, never forget Grandpa. I would like to be just as good a grandpa as he was.

DON   Donnelly, Elfie
       So long, Grandpa

$8.95

DATE			
FEB 12 1988			

87 871